I0768608

Life in a Neon Knapsack

By

Michael Evanichko

Internal and cover illustrations by Thomas Gaadt

KNAPSACK CONTENTS

Acknowledgments

*T*hank you to Thomas Gaadt for bringing this final story in the ***Trilogy of Life*** to life through his stunning illustrations. Thank you to Angel Endicott for breathing life into Martin's story through the wonderful handwritten journal entries. Never-ending thanks to family and friends who inspired stories and situations included in *Life in a Neon Knapsack* as well as its predecessors, *Life in a Supermarket Basket,* and *Life in a Savage Landfill.* The love and support shown over the years helped motivate me to complete the sometimes tedious and maddening tasks of writing and editing. And editing. And editing. And editing.

CHAPTER ONE: MAMIE'S LANDING

Regret and uncertainty smelled like aged wood and tarnished silverware and attacked my senses as I stepped into my recently deceased parent's home. They did a great deal for me in my fifty years on the planet and I sometimes questioned my level of reciprocation. My younger version challenged the belief that children were gifts from God and my rebellious behavior led to a welcomed yet feared disownment. Booted from the house at fourteen would've proved challenging to explore the freedom I desired. Paying rent and grocery shopping at such a young age seemed ridiculous.

An open floor plan exposed the house and a hallway led to three small bedrooms and one tiny bathroom. I scanned the hazy living room and marveled at the concept of a couple owning just one home for the duration of a lifetime. I was currently living in my third house with a fourth possibly coming soon. My parents entered and exited the world in the same town—a town I couldn't wait to flee.

Memories peeked out from every corner. The marathon Uno matches in front of the brick fireplace led my eyes to the nicked wood on the corner of the dinner table. The damaged oak was a courtesy of my front tooth when I was ten. A waist-high brick divider separated the living room from the eat-in kitchen and made home to an assortment of framed pictures. The Blackheads sat on the same furniture through decades of photos, and if we had a family crest, *Frugality,* in a fancy font, would hang above the lion or unicorn or whatever animal Blackhead represented.

"How many Klondike bars have you eaten today, Mamie? If I find another wrapper shoved under the sofa, I am grounding you. You hear me?" my mother said on multiple occasions as she peered at me from the kitchen. She always harped on me about my excessive eating of sweets, but she was also the one stocking our shelves with desserts. My dad used those desserts to motivate me to complete chores. He loved the jingle to the Klondike commercials. "What would you do for a Klondike bar?" he asked. "Would you clean your room? Pull weeds in the garden?" No, neither of those. I would simply reach into the freezer and pull one out. And sometimes that was a chore. Yeah, I was occasionally lazy.

Besides Klondike bars, Little Debbie had tasty snacks, and I fantasized she was my little sister and we shared a bedroom as I shoved her sugary delights down my throat. My nerdy younger brother, Theo, counted the number of snacks in each of Little Debbie's boxes and notified my mother when one went missing. I was always the assumed thief of the snatched cakes. I stood guilty for years until my mom walked in on my dad binge eating a cake from each of the different boxes. He was a sugar thief like me but we needed the escape from my mother's obsession with eating healthy. My brother did not partake in Debbie's delights, for he thought sweets tasted like biodegradable peanuts used for packaging. He was so odd that my folks stopped conceiving after him, clearly scared of a repeated creation.

I opened a few curtains, which brightened the house and showed varying levels of dust over everything. My father passed away in the hospital two and a half weeks ago but he moved to a nursing home six months prior to that, so the house had seen little action for a while. My mother died five years before his nursing home move, and she was the clean freak. My father never retired his coffee mugs to the sink as the rings of corrosion on the decades old end tables proved. Even as my favorite parent, I would have a difficult time living with his lack of regard to cleanliness and organization. I dreaded the thought of emptying the two-car garage; he filled it with so much irrelevant crap it would make a landfill of trash seem like Macy's. I regretted not getting back more when my dad was alone, but he remained fiercely independent even when his mind eroded.

I stepped inside my old bedroom and wondered why my parents never transformed it into a study, or a spare bedroom, or a torture chamber, although I perceived it as a room of torture from ages ten through eighteen. I eventually escaped prison to attend college in a city that wasn't Sundown, Tennessee. It was then I learned another meaning behind the term *sundown;* that it was synonymous with racism and segregation, which disturbed me and made me wonder why the name never changed. Only a few black families lived in Sundown, and I hoped it wasn't a sign of racism. Small town charm was merely backwoods harm, as friendships were scarce and broader horizons were literal.

I opened my bedroom window, and an angry gust of early summer air rustled my old posters, which were still carelessly thumb tacked to the walls. David

Coverdale and his fellow Whitesnake rockers fled the white thumbtacks and the bedroom. They were searching for the redheaded woman from their videos. I pushed the window down to save Duran Duran and Joan Jett. My musical choices diversified as I matured, but you wouldn't see a Kenny Rogers or Reba McEntire poster. Country music was poison I didn't want to swallow in a town neighboring the city most associated with the guitar twangs of country music.

"Mom? Why is Whitesnake in the hall?" asked my daughter, Abigail, as she entered the bedroom with the poster. Her husband, Mateo, followed behind her with my granddaughter riding on his shoulders. Unfortunately, the five-year-old didn't clear the doorway and head-butted the wall like a pro wrestler on fight night. Crying ensued immediately.

"Que carajo estabas pensando!" Abigail said to Mateo as he lowered Sofia and took her into the living room and the wail subsided the further they traveled.

"What'd you say?" I asked, always uncomfortable when they started speaking Spanish. I was proud of my daughter for marrying someone born outside of the United States, as it added a little flair to our family, but communication was sometimes tricky. She had to learn Spanish online with that instructional app named Babbel. I always thought the name of that foreign language learning app was condescending. It implied that prior to learning the language, you babbled incoherently, like a baby.

"What the f-u-c-k were you thinking?" my daughter said, spelling out the four-letter word.

"That seemed a little harsh, dear."

"He just left an imprint of your granddaughter's head on the wall. Harsh? Really, mom? Sofia could have a concussion or even brain damage!" She left the room. I heard her hushing the child and then yelling at Mateo.

I worried the fighting that transpired over the twenty-five years of marriage to my husband, Justin, might've set an unhealthy example for my daughter and my son, Lucas. We tried to be discreet with our arguments when the kids were young, but eventually lost that battle as the curtain dropped and we performed well enough to win Tony Awards. The disconnect in our marriage led to counseling, trial separations, divorce threats, and eventually resulted in Justin fleeing the coop thirteen days ago. He blamed everything on me, all the dysfunction—but I couldn't be the glue that held everything together. Some glues don't sustain the tacky specifications needed to prevent things from falling apart. I lost my husband and my father within weeks of one another.

I opened the closet door and glanced at the clothing of the eighties. A denim jacket with padded shoulders led to a plaid miniskirt and many striped garments; so many stripes it caused vertigo. The frilly baby-blue prom gown muted the stripes and reminded me the three years of high school were capped by a hideous dress.

Given the way I dressed, school was bound to be challenging. My best friend was a fashionista with no fashion sense, and I allowed her to dress me. She called me her muse and I put the muse in amusing.

A black instrument case hid under the gown. My days as a flute player in grade school came to mind. I was never very good, and it wasn't cool to be in the band in high school, so I ditched it—much to my parent's dismay, as flutes weren't cheap. I gave them false hope I'd pick it back up at some point, but then the pressures of high school mounted and I wanted what the popular girls had: the attention, the beauty, the boys.

Something grabbed my leg and I shrieked.

"Hi Nana!" Sofia completed her wailing and wanted some loving. I squatted to her level and my knees popped; my kneecaps wanted to escape the arthritic middle-aged body. Sofia swatted at my left knee. "Pop!" she said. Old and young, we were both damaged goods as she displayed a red circle in the middle of her forehead with a little raised bump. I hugged her tiny body.

"Are you okay, sweetheart?" My interactions with my granddaughter made me feel as old as a cracked tombstone in a centuries-old private cemetery. Being around children aged me and I couldn't make believe I was thirty. She nodded and escaped my clutches, squeezing past me to enter the closet. I allowed her to crawl around under the hanging clothing as I pulled out several tops and recalled how my breasts looked in them. My tiny bosom was hard to highlight in any type of shirt. The vividness of those recollections amazed me as I typically struggled to remember a movie I watched two days prior. Also, what kind of demented human girl wore fuzzy turtlenecks?

Sofia emerged from the realm of ugly clothing with a suitcase of make-up. I used to color my eyelids with purples and pinks and blues, which was ironic as I'm lucky to wear lipstick nowadays.

"Here you go. You can paint on this." I handed Sofia a tablet from my top dresser drawer. She removed three make-up pencils and began drawing on the empty page. Abigail called me and I left the bedroom as Sofia dumped all the make-up out of the bag and continued to create the modern masterpiece she'd begun. My old bedroom would never be the same.

"Where is dad?" Abigail asked.

"No clue. Why? You haven't heard from him?"

"No. I called him two days ago and left a voicemail."

"Who checks voicemails?" I wasn't that hip to the advances in mobile phones, nor did I understand the features on my smart phone, but I knew checking voicemails was a dated activity. Voicemails suffered a fate similar to answering machines in the nineties.

"I texted as well. Nothing. I'm worried. Where did he go?"

"I don't know."

"And you don't care?"

Maybe he returned to Chicago, I told my daughter. Even though our current home was Atlanta, we moved to the windy city after we were married as Justin landed a job as a television producer for an up-and-coming cable station. He had a bunch of friends and colleagues in Chicago.

"Okay, but how could you have not talked to him, Mom? When did you last talk to him?"

I hadn't communicated with him at all since he left thirteen days ago, and I was relieved to have him gone, but I wouldn't share that with Abigail, although she knew we were feuding.

"My dad just died; don't you think I've had other things on my mind? Your father is a big boy. I'm sure he is fine. He was probably just trying to avoid the funeral. You know how much he hates funerals."

"Nobody likes funerals, mom. When's the last time you've heard your friends talking about how they can't wait to see their dearly departed spread out in a wooden box? Gosh, Gertrude, I wonder what Hilda's going to be wearing. Will it be a bit more conservative or slutty?

"Who the hell are Gertrude and Hilda?"

"Look, just call Dad. Right now. Please?"

I rolled my eyes and shot a look of disapproval. Calling Justin was not on my priority list but avoiding that call *was* on my priority list. It was marital war; the kind that signals defeat for the spouse who initiates communication. Abigail always drew the weakness from me. I sighed dramatically and pulled my phone from the back pocket of my jeans. I dialed and hit the speaker button, so I didn't have to talk to him intimately. Talking on speakerphone was a passive aggressive way to disconnect.

Mateo seemed uncomfortable as he turned and headed for the kitchen. His tight jeans hugging his hips like a koala bear hugging a tree. He was that rare creature—a very attractive husband who treated his wife like a queen. Respectful and dedicated, even when my daughter was being a bitch.

"Hello?" Justin answered. "Hello? Are you there, Mamie?"

"She's here, dad. Me too. Where are you? Why haven't you answered my calls?"

"Oh. Hi honey. What are you two doing?"

"We're at granddaddy's house cleaning. Are you okay? Why didn't you attend the funeral?"

A familiar orchestra of sounds filled the background. The secret location of my husband was now exposed as a female voice on a loudspeaker announced the boarding of some randomly numbered flight. He was at the airport!

"Look, I was there in spirit. I really was. I had my own little memorial for Gary. Ouch! That was my foot. That was my broken foot!" Justin said to a stranger at the airport. They apparently ran over his broken foot with a piece of luggage. His stupid foot cracked two months ago when he tripped rushing out the front door. He literally stepped on a crack and instead of breaking his mama's back, he broke his outer metatarsus. And it might never heal. Good for him. I tried not to care that he was possibly doing something fun while I had the laborious task of clearing my parent's home and putting it on the market. A task that would keep me in town much longer than I wanted to be around.

"I have to go. Am I going to hear your voice at all, Mamie? I mean, isn't there anything you want to say to me? Anything at all?"

"Talk to him, mom!"

My lips stayed together as I glanced at Mateo's ass again, and that made me feel good. The little things helped you through life's agony.

"I love you, Abs. I'll call you soon. I gotta run. Ouch! That's my foot! I'm wearing a goddamn boot, can't you see?" Someone else ran over his foot and I almost laughed until I heard a female voice asking if he was okay, *baby*. Baby. Certainly, the stranger who ran over his foot would not be calling him *baby*. Who called him baby, and where was he going with this person who called him baby?

I hit the 'end' button and concluded the charade. A cloud of discomfort floated between my gaze with Abigail. She heard *baby* as well and was processing the repercussions. She was judging her father for being a bad husband and father. I was off the hook—for now.

"What are you doing back there, Sofia?"

Abby left me alone and I looked at Mateo who opened kitchen cabinets, checking for one large enough to hide to escape his wife's drama.

Baby?

I didn't care if Justin was fleeing Atlanta with a hoochie mama. Or maybe he was returning to Atlanta with a hoochie mama he met on some exotic vacation he'd been on for the last thirteen days. I still had nothing to say.

"Can we have this?" Mateo was holding a white, porcelain gravy boat in the shape of a kitten. Someone aptly named it *The Puking Kitten*, and it was a gag gift my folks received many years ago. It was hideous, and giving it away saved me from handling one more item.

"Sold! For the stunningly affordable price of nothing!" I said as Mateo smiled in a sexy manner, exposing his polished, white teeth. My eyes lowered to the tightness in front of his pants until I realized the inappropriateness of the glance.

"Mom!" Abigail reentered the room. I was cold busted for checking out my son-in-law or I was going to be reprimanded for allowing *cold busted* to enter my thoughts. My daughter was a sixth grade English teacher and didn't approve of slang from the Urban Dictionary.

"Yes, you may have the Puking Kitten," I said to Mateo to deflect the possible incarceration, and I turned to Abigail. "Yes, dear?"

She grabbed my hand and pulled me into my old bedroom. "What is this?" she asked, pointing at the neon green knapsack lying on my old twin bed; the contents spread out and currently being inspected by Sofia. "This was in that bag." She handed me a hunting knife in its protective leather sheath. I forgot the backpack was in the closet; I hadn't seen that bag and its contents for decades, but the memories of it and its contents never left my mind.

"Okay, let's put everything back, please." I began shoving things back into the ripped, stained bag, grabbing a journal from Sofia's hand rather aggressively.

"Mom, calm down. Was this your bag? Grandma allowed you to have a knife like that?"

"No. It wasn't mine."

"Where did it come from then? There is still blood on the knife. How old is this stuff?"

I never shared the story of that summer with my children. Even if I wanted to share, I couldn't. I was sworn to secrecy.

"Jesus, Abigail. Can we just forget about this? If we have to discuss everything we find while we're emptying this house, this process will take forever."

The explosion entered my head.

I tried to hide my trembling hands by quickly shoving the contents back inside the knapsack. Abigail grabbed Sofia's shoulder and led her out of the bedroom, her face scrunched as she glanced at me on the way out. My odd behavior and refusal to discuss the bag puzzled her. She would not drop it either. I needed to devise a simple lie, or I needed to tell the story of that fateful summer of 1986.

I was fifteen and everything I thought I knew about myself was about to explode like the plane in the sky above me.

CHAPTER TWO: EXPLODING DISCONTENT

"Are you sleeping here?" Abigail asked. She and her family were preparing to leave for the day, having boxed a considerable amount of kitchen items and only breaking three pieces of tableware, including *The Sharing Plate*, which was never shared by my mother because she never understood the idea. It was given to us by a neighbor during a summer cookout and the customary duty was to pass the plate to another family. The only sharing occurred within my family as we passed the loaded plate of food around the table on major holidays or special occasions.

This plate has no owner, for its journey never ends. Its purpose is a special one, for the love and joy it sends. The food upon this plate was made with tenderness and care. It passes love from home to home for everyone to share...

Sadly, the plate's journey ended rather abruptly, much like my mother's life. A heart attack took her at seventy-one. It shocked all of us because her health was decent. An occasional medication for high blood pressure and recommendations for weight loss (she wasn't as strict about eating healthy later in life) were the only mild health issues documented, but she always complied.

My dad discovered my mom's lifeless body on the bathroom floor. After running water for a bath in the claw-footed antique tub she dropped to the floor after cardiac arrest. He tried to resuscitate her but it was too late and he beat himself up for not hearing her fall and for not checking on her earlier, convinced if he had, she would still be alive. His Alzheimer symptoms began shortly after her death. He spent most days glued to his recliner watching repeated news telecasts as well as Gunsmoke and Andy Griffith reruns. The one good thing that emerged from the deterioration of his mind was that he forgot my mom was dead and that he blamed himself for her demise. Helen Mirren and John Lithgow would convey the goofy and the dramatic elements of my parent's love story with pizazz, but someone needed to write the award-winning screenplay.

Abigail stood at the door, still waiting for my response.

"Yes. Yes, I'm sorry, I am staying here."

"Are you sure, mom? It's filthy here. The hotel is only twenty minutes away and you'll get a much better sleep."

"Maybe she wants to reminisce, Abby," Mateo said softly. I kept my eyes above his waist as I smiled and made eye contact. He was correct, though. I was about to embark on a journey through my past and I needed to stay in the house where it all began—it was essential to the integrity of the recollections.

I kissed Sofia goodbye, her forehead now looking like a bullseye. She waited by the front door as I hugged my daughter and then Mateo. He wrapped his brawny arms around me and squeezed a bit of comfort into me, and then the three of them disappeared into the night, heading to a hotel in a neighboring small town.

Baby.

That female voice from the phone call with my husband had my mind racing. Although our relationship had been an amusement park ride—the old wooden roller coaster that almost gave you a concussion—as far as I knew, he never strayed with another woman, and I never cheated on him. Suddenly, the need for the truth pushed on my brain and I needed the answer before the pressure caused an acute subdural hematoma. I picked up my phone and called my long-lost husband as I moved to the kitchen. As the phone rang, I pulled a bottle of vodka from the back of the stinky freezer. By the time I poured a few gulps in a glass, the call went to his voicemail. His recorded greeting, "Not Bieber, not Timberlake. The even cooler Justin cannot pleasure you with his voice. Please say something I actually want to hear, and I might call you back." I smirked and rolled my eyes; he was such a huge dork sometimes. I missed his dorkiness, which prompted me to call two more times but didn't get the pleasure of his voice. I didn't leave a message, as he might be on a plane. I needed to drink and relieve the pressure on my brain and unpacking the neon knapsack was just the thing to distract me from my marital woes.

My former bedroom and the entire house were modest. My brother and I grew up knowing everything about one another, like conjoined twins, never able to detach because my folks could not afford the separation surgery. Their jobs prevented them from affording a bigger house or a luxury item of any sort. In the small middle-Tennessean town, the career path veered off the treacherous Calfkiller highway—that twisting and turning stretch of road where motorcycle enthusiasts enjoyed tempting fate; where one wrong turn made you part of the scenic view until the paramedics scraped your face off a pine tree and separated the rest of your body from a cluster of kindling.

My mom stocked shelves at K-Mart and eventually worked up to management, which was better pay but tougher to stomach. Working with the public was intolerable and eventually led her to quit the retail giant, only to start over again stocking shelves in the freezer at Sam's Club. She liked that gig much more because it required her to get decked out in black bibs with a ski mask, which allowed her to move about incognito and avoid the public. Jobs were scarce in Sundown, so her travel time to work was lengthy, which allowed Theo and me a temporary escape from her rules and regulations. We did nothing helpful around the house unless she was breathing down our necks, and she reminded us of our uselessness daily. Theo fared better because he told her how pretty she looked or commented on her weight.

My father was a mechanic. He worked on farm equipment; namely the enormous Big Bud 747 farm tractors, and I sometimes got to ride them with him. The satisfaction he got when his days of repairs paid off and the monsters ran without blowing up was a beauty to behold. But I beheld them only as a child; at age fifteen, those gigantic robot farmers stopped exciting me and I feared being spotted in them with my daddy, for it reeked of lameness. The last time my father offered me a ride on a Big Bud 747 was the day of the explosion, the day the neon green knapsack packed with intrigue came into my life.

I pulled the bag out of my old closet and unzipped the oval opening. I emptied the contents onto the bed, as Sofia did, and reached for my glass of vodka on the dresser. I wanted to start at the beginning and not jump around in the timeline. No fancy narration like those independent films purchased from fancy film festivals. I wanted to work my mind through the first steps taken in those days when I was fifteen years old and my life seemed totally dramatic. The days when girls wanted to die because of a broken fingernail.

I quickly learned the meaning of genuine drama.

"Can you please just go," my mother said to my dad. The school bus would pull up in front of our house soon, and my mom was getting our lunches ready. She wanted him out of her way and out of her face. An edge, or tension, sometimes surrounded them, but it wasn't as frequent as the last two months. The new norm of their interactions was like a box of Saltines and not the low-sodium variety. Eavesdropping never revealed misdeeds from either party, so I concluded they had finally grown tired of the habits that used to be mild annoyances—bad habits that were no longer overlooked. For example, my dad never picked up after himself. He took his muddy boots and his stinky socks off and left them next to his recliner. He never touched the socks and only moved the boots when he needed them on his feet again. Three weeks ago, my mom hurled one of them at him while he walked to the bathroom. The crusty boot hit him in the back and the dried dirt created a cloud of dust.

"Why the hell did you do that for?"

"I'm sorry. I didn't mean to hit you. I was just tossing them towards the closet," she said. She didn't feel the need to nag about it for the hundredth time. She hoped passive-aggressive violence might fix the problem.

It didn't.

The biggest thing that bugged my dad about my mom was her perfectionism. And her obsession with healthy eating. The traditional, battered-dipped fish and chips never made it to our table. Lemon pepper grilled fish and mixed vegetables took up permanent residence on that table. She couldn't control his Big Mac urges during the workdays, though, so he ate poorly while away from home and had the diabetes and belly to prove it. He claimed to eat salads for lunch when she didn't pack him leftovers, but I knew he was full of baloney. My mother believed him, which prompted me to roll my eyes.

I rolled my eyes a lot, which led to anxiety over the possibility I'd gain a wonky eye when older—like my grandfather. He once yelled at me for not looking at him when he spoke to me, but when I tried to connect my eyes to his, I feared my eyeballs would explode. I never knew which eye was looking at me. It frightened me and I had nightmares that one day my eyes would start doing their own thing and I would scare the hell out of my grandchildren, too. But I had a solution to prevent permanent mental damages—I'd only have conversations with them in a dark room, or through a bathroom door. Or I could wear those obnoxiously huge plastic sunglasses my parents wore after an eye doctor visit.

"I'm going. Don't ya worry, sweetheart. You won't see me all damn day. How late do ya work?" he asked, stopping at the door to await a response.

"I close tonight. Won't be home until ten thirty or eleven."

"Well then, you won't see me all night, either."

"Yes. I know that. Make sure you eat the chicken and rice I made last night. It's in the aluminum container. Pop it in the oven on three seventy-five for forty-five minutes."

She prepped food in disposable aluminum containers because she knew my dad wouldn't wash a used casserole dish. At least not correctly. She once sliced her index finger on a chunk of hardened ham still stuck to the inside of a dish that my dad supposedly washed a week earlier. The injury required three stitches. It was totally the most obnoxious waste of blood ever.

"You can add cheese for the last five minutes," she said.

"Cheese. How special is that fer us? That's lotsa calories. We need to puke it up after dinner then?" he asked as he stepped into the garage. He chuckled before the door slammed behind him. He didn't slam it himself—the springs went out of whack and my mother nagged him for months to replace the mechanism.

"Asshole," she said under her breath, but I heard it from my room. I felt another tantrum brewing within my soul about how stupid it was to live in a doll house. The last eruption ended with my mom, dad and brother all telling me to move in with my best friend, Devisha. Her brother was off at college, and they had an extra room in their split-level mansion.

My brother finally stepped out of the bathroom, his skinny, fourteen-year-old frame clearly suffering from healthy eating. My fifteen-year-old body suffered from disproportion. I had the breasts of a pregnant hamster, or as the popular girls in school called them, "titter tots". My ass was the same size as my equally unpopular black best friend, Devisha. When we walked down the hall together, our rumps looked like a pair of coconuts sashaying in the tropical winds. We only wished we were on a tropical island instead of high school. My classmates joked that I only befriended Devisha because of our matching bubble butts, and this simply wasn't true—our friendship began before our asses grew into sashaying coconuts. She was the only black girl in our high school, which made her an outcast, and outcasts often had zero friends. She offered me an Oreo cookie at lunch in the third grade, and a beautiful friendship was born.

"It's all yours," Theodore said as he passed me. I could smell the ripe aroma of the deuce he dropped, yet the exhaust fan wasn't running. I didn't understand his obsession with smelling his own body rot. He totally enjoyed smelling his farts, too; my brother gave vivid meaning to *gag me with a spoon*. I held my breath and flipped the fan switch and walked to the kitchen and sat, waiting for the smell to vanish. It typically took three to five minutes.

"Why aren't you moving? The bus will be here in five minutes," my mother said to me, with that unnecessary tone I heard all too often. Our relationship was straight off the tennis court—I typically won a bunch of points, but she always won the match.

"Yeah, well, this butt-wad hogged the bathroom and stunk it up. I'm not going in there just yet." I looked at Theo, sitting to my right. "Why is it so hard to put the fan on?"

"Theodore, please be considerate. Your sister is right. I can smell it out here."

Theodore ignored us and opened his math book, pretending to read about equations and expressions. "You should at least have your school clothes on, Mamie," my mother said as she practiced a different type of mathematical expression referred to as D=NM² or *Daughter suffering from a Nagging Mother- doubled.*

"Umm, I do."

"You're wearing *that* to school?"

"You're wearing *that* to work?" I knew it sounded harsh, but tennis was a tough sport—only the strong survived. But how dare she criticize my denim mini skirt and yellow tank top? She wanted me to fit in with the other girlies in school and my ensemble would achieve this fit perfectly. Years later I realized my thinking was incorrect.

"I'm not wearing this to work. I don't go in for three more hours. I get to relax in these sweatpants after you two leave. And don't be so sassy, young lady, or I'll ground you all summer!"

I was scheduled to work three days a week at the local swimming pool's concession stand beginning Monday. I was already grounded for the summer. My eyes would lose the ability to see clearly after witnessing all the gross skin that Sundown's predominately unfit folks would display. School would be done, though, on the positive side. With only three days of school left, I already felt freedom from annoying teachers and classes and homework and tests. And classmates from hell.

"Hey mom. Can Charlie sleep over on Friday?" Theo asked.

That was not ideal for me. I hated my brother's toad friend. He was scaly and stinky and peed his pants.

That's why I called him a toad, because anytime you grabbed one of those hop-a-longs they pissed all over you.

"I have to work all weekend," my mother said.

"He's only staying Friday." Theo sometimes talked slow and whiny—especially when he wanted something he knew was difficult to get. A minute later he finished and he only spoke a six word sentence. Although he sounded mentally slow, he was sharp as a tack, but he struggled with communication. Typical nerd, I supposed.

"Ask your dad tonight. Mamie, why are you still sitting? Go finish getting ready!"

I stood and headed for the bathroom. The air in there had returned to normal—if you called fake flowers with expired deodorizer sticks hiding between the petals, normal.

"The bus is here, Mamie! Come on!" my mom said from the other side of the door before I even had the cap off the toothpaste tube or squatted on the toilet.

Twenty minutes later, I smoked a joint while walking down the gravel and dirt path that ran parallel to the main road. The high schoolers dubbed the path *Sex Lane* because many students got it on in the woods that ran the length of the path. Since Sundown High School was only a mile away, it was easy to sneak back there during lunch or after school. I sometimes saw dried up condoms hanging in the weeds, almost displayed as a bragging right, and it grossed me out. Besides that, I preferred the path over riding in that obnoxious, filthy school bus every day with those idiot boys. They enjoyed sticking their fingers up the narrow gap where the seat and back cushions joined. I once gave a boy a bloody nose after he stuck a lollipop stick up there and it almost pierced my butt.

A few feet ahead I spotted a threesome of cellophane birthday balloons stuck in a tree, about twenty feet up. The branches of the tree held the balloons like a mother cradling her newborn child. I stopped for a moment and stared at them. Their pinks and blues and silvers reflected the morning sun rising behind me. The roach I just smoked was working my imagination and I pondered the story of the balloons. How did they escape and to whom did they belong to before floating away—a journey that proved fatal to the festive party favors. Did they brighten the day for a child or an elder? Was it a happy birthday or an unhappy birthday? Two of the three of them were halfway deflated, which made me sad. The life was nearly gone for the shiny objects of happiness. Or sadness. Or discontent. My altered mind wanted to pause and create a dramatic tale, but it was time to move on or I'd be late for my third to the last day of the crapfest called school.

I walked two steps and was pushed to the ground by an unseen force. My knees dug into an assortment of stones and chards of glass, and I regretted wearing a miniskirt. An explosion penetrated my ear canals, comparable to the loudest clap of thunder I ever heard multiplied by a hundred.

The ground vibrated and the trees rattled, and my first instinct was to laugh about how good the pot was to land me in the middle of a Steven Spielberg movie.

And then I looked up and wished it was make believe.

Or that the pot I just inhaled truly was the good shit.

CHAPTER THREE: A BLOODY HIGH

I took a couple gulps of vodka and slid off the side of the bed, gently landing on my now much smaller butt. I encountered the same bullshit most women experienced with body insecurities and dysmorphia throughout most of my life. Every year seemed to bring about a different goal or strategy for losing weight or firming my hips or losing arm flab. Juice cleanses taunted me several times a year, and I once embarked on a seven-day cleanse, much to my husband's annoyance. I took the week off from cooking, as I wanted to avoid the temptation to sneak a bite of something while preparing.

Justin pouted a full seven days for having to play chef and punished me by refraining from sex. I wanted to lose my panties twice that week because I felt so light and clean and attractive. Juice cleanses are amazing for the libido, but you must have a willing participant. The only willing participant I had was Beek, my vibrator that was named after James Van Der Beek. That angsty Dawson dude was the trigger I needed to achieve sexual satisfaction.

The week was a success. I lost ten pounds of total body weight and my waist was two inches smaller. And when Justin decided he wanted to take a ride on the love train, I derailed it with a migraine. The excuse was incredibly lame and the games we played were so childish that I wondered how our marriage survived. It proved difficult to prevent high school sweethearts from becoming middle-aged sour grapes, and I tired of the struggles through the years. We met in grade school but my love for him didn't ignite until I startled him sitting on the toilet at a high school party two days after I found the knapsack. He had me at *pass the toilet paper, please*.

I smiled and swigged the vodka and the burn down my throat made my eyes water just like I needed them to do on the way to school that fateful day.

I was on my bloody knees again, after the explosion.

It had to be more than smoking potent weed. I never experienced an earthquake nor was I involved in any other of mother nature's deadly temper tantrums. Blood trickled to my shoes as I stood and looked to the sky to catch a display of fireworks minus the brilliant sparkles of colors. I thanked the gods that being high as a kite wasn't literal as I wanted far from the mess above. A gigantic cloud of smoke was in the center and small unidentified objects zig-zagged from the puffs. That wasn't an earthquake. There were no winds or darkness or continuing thunder. Something exploded in the sky, and it was raining the body of that something. The cloud of smoke cleared a bit and I saw distinct square and rod shapes raining down and all around.

I was struck on my forehead and pushed back to the ground, this time landing on my butt. Pings and pangs of falling debris pierced the dirt around me and the fear of being struck again forced me to my feet and into the woods to find protection in the trees. I crouched under an enormous pine tree and wiped blood from my left eye. It came from the gash in my forehead and I was suddenly convinced someone wanted me dead—I was being attacked and I didn't know why. Maybe my mother sent out a group of snipers to rid the world of me because she hated my outfit, or because I sassed her just minutes ago. A Gila monster would crawl out of the brush if the snipers failed to murder me. It was an inconvenient time to be buzzed.

As I huddled and the metallic shower slowed, I understood I wasn't in the throes of death from a hit placed on me by my mother. I remembered the path to school was below the flight path to the small airport on the other side of Sundown.

The explosion above was a plane.

The surrounding path and woods were littered with plane parts, and I shuddered to think they were also littered with human parts. I didn't see any gore, but how could there not be? The planes that typically appeared overhead were small and fewer people could fit in them, but even if there were no passengers, there would at least be a pilot.

The iron shower stopped but a significant amount of smoke ventured down into the woods. The intense smell of burning pine caused me to cough and gag. Any reasonably sane kid would've raced home screaming and crying but I was more reasonably insane. Curiosity possessed me like the devil trying to come back to earth through a little girl, and when I spotted something shiny a hundred feet ahead, I had to investigate. The smoke scattered as I approached the shine and the muffled sound of sirens echoed in the distance. Cops and ambulances were sure to arrive soon, and I didn't want to be discovered in the area so I quickened my pace as my knees and my head still dripped blood.

The shine that caught my interest belonged to a metal leg with a large black wheel attached. As I reached for it, I felt heat oozing and stopped short of grabbing it because I didn't want to add a scolded hand to the list of the injuries gained within the last few minutes of my young life. The rubber wheel smoldered and the smell ignited a coughing fit.

I scanned the area like The Terminator, my morbid curiosity searching for plane parts. My gaze stopped three trees away and I swore I heard the beeps and saw the red lights that appeared in Arnold Schwarzenegger's head. A neon green object was hanging in the tree and the bright green clashed with the natural green of the tree's leaves. It reminded me of those visual puzzles as a child, the *which one doesn't belong here*, quizzes. I rushed to the tree and saw a knapsack and it hung fifteen feet above my head.

I couldn't explain the intense need to have that bag and to risk being caught by a local police officer. Tampering with evidence at the scene of an accident could spell big trouble but I climbed the tree regardless, grimacing at the pain when I bent my knees. I scaled that tree like a tree-scaling pro and grabbed the backpack and hopped down. I switched on Arnold's scanning robot brain again and saw a blood stain, two minor rips and a black burn stain, but besides that the bag was completely intact. I put my arms into the straps and the bag rested on my back perfectly.

Sirens were closer.

I rushed out of that forest and stumbled back onto the dusty path only to discover what I secretly hoped to see in the woods: a bloody body part. It was half a hand and the thumb and pointer were the only two fingers still attached. The fingernails were long and yellow and I had a sick feeling that I was struck by the stump and the fingernail was the weapon that pierced my forehead just minutes earlier. I covered my mouth and gasped at the thought, grateful to have a fully intact hand and five fingers as I stepped over the carnage and jogged toward school. Shock visited me as my head spun from the pain and the pot and the unreal situation. Heading in the other direction to my house made more sense, but I didn't want to be interrogated by my mother. Besides, hiding the bag that fell from the sky in my school locker would be easier.

Twenty minutes later, I stepped into the school and heard the voice of Principal Alcott desperately urging all students to proceed to their homerooms. The sound of sirens had followed me on the journey to the school and poured into the hallway as I quickly stopped at my locker and stashed the bloody bag.

"What happened to you?" Andy asked. For a second I forgot about the blood trickling down my knees. Andy was the real life geek from the movie Sixteen Candles, but I refused to give him my panties. His pursuit of me started two years ago and he appeared around every corner to strike up a conversation between periods. I told him I fell and rushed to the girl's restroom to clean myself. I was still stoned but needed to be as cool as a cucumber so nobody suspected. I also needed drops for my dried eyeballs—or someone to tell me I had a huge ass, or that I was ugly or something, so I could cry and self-lubricate.

"What happened to you?" asked another concerned student—this time it was Tanya, the girl who sat behind me in English and snickered every time I answered a question. Tanya seemed to think every answer I gave was incorrect, even though the teacher was satisfied with the responses. She was part of the popular group and I didn't own a membership card, so I had no use for her. She might help me self-lubricate, though. I wanted her to look at me with disgust.

"I fell."

"Let me help." Tanya wet a hand towel and dabbed at my forehead. I was stunned that she was helping me but tried not to be transparent. She was the same bitch that pointed and rolled her eyes and laughed at me and Devisha for reasons unknown. She was so deliberate, too, like she didn't care if we saw her pointing. "Rumor has it a plane crashed. Richie Teach saw it explode in the sky. Did you see anything?"

"No." I felt guilty about taking the backpack, or knapsack, as my mother called those kinds of bags, but I couldn't wait to examine the contents, especially if it came from the plane. But why didn't the bag explode to pieces like everything else? Surely it hadn't been hanging in that tree before the explosion, like the deflated birthday balloons. The severed chunk of hand slapped my lying face and forced me to close my eyes and shake my head until the vision dissolved. Fortunately, Tanya thought I was wincing as she dabbed my forehead wound.

"I don't think you'll need stitches. My mother is a nurse and I have a pretty good feeling about this. You can go see the school nurse if you don't believe me."

I looked in the mirror and agreed with amateur nurse Tanya. The cut didn't appear too deep. What a wild story I could share about the hand attacking me, but she wouldn't believe me and then it would get around school that I made up a horrible lie about someone who died in the explosion. As I thought out the implications of honesty, Tanya squatted and began cleaning my knees. The girl who hated my guts was taking care of me! What a bizarre morning. Maybe she would help me self-lubricate after all, only tears of joy. Major plot twist.

"We ask that you head to homeroom immediately. We need to take attendance as soon as possible. Please proceed to your classroom immediately," Principal Alcott said as Nurse Tanya pulled a shard of glass from my right knee.

"You fall on a bottle or something?"

"I don't think so," I said and actually winced this time. She held up another small, yet damaging piece of glass. It felt like something unique and special was happening between us and I wanted to initiate another topic of conversation rather than just answering her questions, but I couldn't think of anything we might have in common. What was the point, anyway? I was sure that once we left the bathroom the moment would be forgotten and she would go back to being a pretentious bitch.

"Are you going to be a nurse, too?" I asked, settling on a topic.

"Maybe. A nurse or a lawyer. My dad's a lawyer. Do I want to take after my mom or my dad? Which one do I want to make happy? It's a great position to be in because they both want me to follow in their footsteps, so they both give me anything I ask for or do anything I ask them to do. Also, I'm an only child," she said, well on her return to pretentious bitch status. I winced again as she popped out another piece of glass. Maybe I *had* fallen on a bottle. "How about you? If you had to follow in the footsteps of your mom or your dad, who would it be and what would be your career?"

Why had I opened my stupid mouth. Do I tell her I long to take after my mother and stock frozen tilapia and stuffed mushroom appetizers in a freezer? Or am I taking after my dad and crawling around under farm equipment? Either career involved the same wardrobe. I was horrified of passing a mirror wearing insulated bib overalls. My delay in answering led me to fear she would believe I was lying.

"Physical therapist. My mom," I blurted, not knowing why that was my choice. Probably because Devisha's mother was a physical therapist.

"That's a good one. But I thought your mom stocked shelves in the freezer at Sam's Club? My mom was shopping there a couple of weeks ago and couldn't find those two-hundred-pound bags of chicken. She had to open the freezer door and yell for help. She said your mom popped her head out and scared the crap out of her."

I chuckled and hoped it didn't sound like the nervous chuckle it was.

"Yeah, well, she's studying to be a physical therapist, and working that job during the day," I said, impressed with the answer I pulled out of my big ass crack.

"If you choose your dad's career, what would you be doing?"

Shit. I couldn't pause too long. I just needed to blurt-

"Making ties."

"Ties?"

"Designing ties. You know, the fancy ties the business guys wear. My dad designs the patterns. I like to draw, so I think I would be good at that."

"Hmmm. Your dad has a side job, too? I know he fixed my uncle's tractor a couple of weeks ago. I thought he was a mechanic?" She was testing me, clearly, and I was failing the test miserably.

"Yes. The mechanic is the side job. His main job is designing ties." The tie job came to my brain because tie rhymes with die which is what I wanted to do at that point.

"I think you're good. You really should be more careful out there. Did you trip getting off the bus?"

I told her I was daydreaming and tripped over a rock while walking to school. Our friendship was completely based on lies and had a wonderful future; I was sure of that.

"So, then you saw the explosion?"

"No. I heard something, though," I said but wanted to scream. She was the most intuitive person ever. She was pushing me to hell by asking so many intrusive questions.

Principal Alcott made another announcement and I thanked Tanya for her help and wished her luck with her career as a nurse if she chose that option, even though I would see her a zillion more times before we graduated and would write the sentiment in her yearbook along with *stay cool*. She laughed and said it was too early to decide and that she would continue to manipulate her parents to get what she wanted. I wished I could manipulate my parents, but what could I get from them? A quart of hydraulic fluid? A box of frozen crab legs?

I hated my life. I needed the knapsack.

As I raced down the deserted halls of the school, I wondered how Tanya would treat me around her snobby friends. I thought about her introduction of me as her bestie. Suddenly, the devastation and horror of an exploding plane and dead passengers took the back seat to my desire for popularity.

"Mamie Blackhead. Mamie Blackhead?" I heard as I approached my homeroom door.

"Here!" I said as I entered the room and Mrs. Kent eyed me suspiciously. I sat next to Devisha.

"Where you been? What happened to you?" Devisha looked at my injured forehead as I felt a drop of blood trickle down. The trickling red shit from my body was beginning to annoy me. I dabbed it with a towel I had grabbed from the restroom.

I shared everything about my life with Devisha and loved her dramatic reactions for the most mundane stories. She would lose her shit when I shared the explosion and the bag and Tanya.

Mrs. Kent hushed us as Principal Alcott's voice yet again erupted from the speaker above our heads. He informed us about the explosion and that it was being investigated. He really didn't know if it was a plane or a car or a farmhouse that burst. His main concern was the safety of all students and that everyone was accounted for and that classes would continue as he felt it would be safer for everyone to remain under the school roof rather than venture out onto the site while it was under investigation. *Too late, I already did that.*

The bell rang a short while later and I dragged Devisha to my locker to show her the knapsack. I had briefed her on my adventure during homeroom.

"Open it," she said.

"Now?"

"Real quick. Just to look real quick. We do not know what's in there. Just do it, come on!" I unzipped the oval top and spread the flaps and reached my hand inside. The first item I felt and pulled out was an orange and white striped collar with a metal name tag dangling from it. I held it up and read the name aloud, "Bow. B-O-W."

"Bow? Like Bow-wow?"

"Bow, like Bo, I think. And look, there's still white fur stuck to it."

Suddenly, a voice yelled out in the crowded hallway.

"Plane crash. Certified plane crash. It's on the Nashville news. They're trying to figure out how many people were on board." The guy who was yelling this information emerged from the hallway crowd with his football letterman jacket on, an unusual article of clothing to be wearing at the beginning of summer. What a bragger.

It was my future husband, Justin Whitney.

He was holding the hand of Tanya as they strolled down the hallway. I hadn't realized they were an item, nor did I really care, since Justin didn't know I existed. He was cute, though, with his feathered blond hair and blue eyes and that firm, athletic body. I would've let him kiss me with tongue and I would've kissed back. Something I hadn't done at that point in my life. Lips had touched mine a couple times, but I pulled away before too much slobber happened, so that didn't count as a kiss.

As the power couple passed me and Devisha, they stopped and Justin made one last announcement before they disappeared into the crowd again.

"Oh, and there were no survivors."

CHAPTER FOUR: WAITING FOR CHICHI

Thirty-five years later, I thought about Justin's announcement that everyone died on the plane and I remembered how it suddenly made everything I had experienced that morning as real as the black-and-white checkered floor under my feet. It took someone else acknowledging that it was true, even though I saw the debris. I transplanted onto the doomed plane and heard a pilot screaming about the engine catching on fire as turbulence smacked the plane around. I grabbed the hand of a passenger next to me right before the blast. And then I no longer existed. My imagination was in overdrive that morning.

I held the faded orange dog collar for a moment and then tossed it on the bed. My glass was empty and it felt like a crime. I needed a refill, stat. I almost gave up the liquor, successfully quitting for three months until the one-two punch that was Justin and my dad happened and vodka reentered my life. I occasionally required booze to stay healthy. Wine relaxed me and helped me sleep. Vodka and rum removed the edge and gave me a pleasant disposition. Early in our marriage, Justin told me I was more fun when I was drinking and I never shared with him I needed to drink to manage his idiocy.

He once shot a nail halfway through his finger with a nail gun—that called for a vodka and soda water with a squirt of lemon juice. I had sympathy and realized accidents happened but I warned him several times to keep his left hand a safe distance from the nail gun. Instead of rushing to the emergency room to have the nail removed, he flipped his finger over, grabbed a hammer and pounded the metal out of his finger, much like ridding a strip of floor trim of nails after ripping it off the wall.

He once confronted a cashier at Target, convinced she never returned his credit card after scanning his order. When she denied she had the card, he insinuated she was a liar, which made the young girl cry and then quit on the spot. She threw her smock at him on her way out. He later found the card in his back pocket. That incident required a shot of bourbon, followed by a lime margarita on the rocks minus the nasty salt, please. I finished the night with a glass of merlot. I had to numb the dumb and diminish the feel to kill.

He once forgot our anniversary even after I darkened the date on the kitchen calendar and drew a cake in the square. He also went out after work with his buddies and didn't get home until midnight. I drank rum and cokes alone that night after the kids went to bed.

Aggravations aside, he was the love of my life and the only guy with whom I shared a deep connection, both physically and emotionally. Even though I obsessed over his negative attributes he was a patient and understanding partner. I've been attracted to other men, most of them appearing in the hotels I've managed during my career in the hospitality industry, but they were emotionally unavailable, which was a good thing. Justin had a great heart and was a great provider, and I knew he was committed to me and our children, and I never worried about infidelity.

Until now.

I let him walk out, knowing I would need his emotional support when my father passed, but I figured he would be gone a few hours not a couple weeks. Our partnership was damaged if he had another woman. I wasn't sure an affair was excusable.

As I poured more vodka into my glass the telephone rang and surprised me and I spilled the drink onto the counter. I had forgotten my parents still owned a landline and the sound of the ring was foreign. My mom refused a mobile phone of her own, so she and my dad shared a flip phone. The advanced technological world frightened them, preventing the smart phone upgrade.

The microwave clock flashed 10:32 and I wondered who was calling so late.

"Hello? Hello?" I said, hearing breathing.

"Is Gary home?" an older man asked and I dreaded sharing the news that my father was no longer alive. I recalled my mother taking the same calls years ago when my grandmother passed, which always led her to hysterics.

"May I ask who's calling?"

"Chuck."

"Chuck, hello! It's Mamie, Gary's daughter," I said. Chuck was an old neighbor and friend of my dad's who moved away decades ago, shortly after I left town. "I'm sorry to tell you this, but-,"

"Gary is gone, isn't he?" Chuck guessed.

"Yes, I'm sorry. He'd been staying at Walton Manor; his dementia got the best of him."

Silence.

"You still there, Chuck?"

"Yes. I'm-," his voice tapered to silence, and I could hear sniffling. "Gary was a remarkable man, you know?" More sniffling and sobbing. I felt sorry for

Chuck. He was a great friend, and I knew it hurt my dad when he moved to the west coast. Chuck was a musician and got a job at a college, teaching music. He always seemed the odd one about town, never dating or getting married and having kids.

"He loved you, Chuck. We were all sad when you moved. Are you still in California?"

"Yes. I'm still here. Retired. I was actually calling to see if I could come visit Gary. We lost touch after your mom passed. I should've come back, but I was transitioning out of teaching. I was training my replacement. It was a crazy time."

"I'm sure dad understood."

"Are you clearing the house now? Is that why you're there? Or did you move back?"

"It's been a couple weeks since he passed, and yes, I'm here to clean the house, get rid of stuff. And as you know, there is a bunch here. Especially in the garage." I laughed, and he chuckled as well, knowing what a hoarder my dad was.

"I wonder, Mamie, is that mounted trout I had made for your dad still in the house?"

I spotted it on the wall above the sofa. It had been there so long it became part of the wall, along with paintings and senior pictures and family pictures and sconces. If the walls could talk, they would scream for independence.

"Yes. It is," I said, noticing a layer of dust covering the body of the fish. It was literally swimming in dust. "Would you like it?"

"I would love to have it. Can I give you my address? I'll pay you for it," he said. I wrote his address and assured him that payment would not be necessary. He told me he still played guitar and piano and occasionally performed at a pub in his small, college town and after we said goodbye a wave of sadness hit me. How could he be healthy, both physically and mentally, yet both my parents were dead—they were all the same ages? That seemed unfair. I grabbed my drink and headed back to the bedroom and the knapsack.

"Do you want to take another ride with me?" my dad asked when I got home from school the day of the explosion. It was business as usual for him and he needed to repair another piece of farm equipment. Besides the acknowledgement that the plane accident happened, he wasn't talking about the extraordinary event in detail even though the tragedy occurred just a half mile from our house. I was eager to watch the news to learn more about what happened. It was strange to be connected to something so major but not share the story with my family. I was happy I could confide in Devisha.

"What's wrong with yer forehead?"

My head was leaking again. I ended up seeing the school nurse about my wounds when they continued to bleed during the school day. I was honest about what happened and I shared my whereabouts at the time of the crash and asked for confidentiality. Nurse Paula chuckled and told me we had patient-client confidentiality and my secret was safe. I also shared that I found a bag and I would take it to the police station. That neon bag I swiped from the tree was still in my locker and that was the best hiding place for it. It would be hard to camouflage in our miniature house but I also had to be weary at school, too. Neon knapsacks were not popular with my classmates. Trapper Keepers and lunch boxes were all the rage. I retired my Charlie's Angels lunchbox when I hit junior high but some high schoolers still used them.

"I tripped on the gravel on my way to school. You know I had just made it to school when the plane crashed," I said, hoping to avoid being asked if I saw the plane.

"It didn't crash. It exploded in mid-air. Bad thang. That has always been my fear about living this close to the airport. I know it's a tiny airport, but all it takes is a tiny, ole plane to land on our house to kill us all."

"Wow, dad. Can you be any gloomier?" I asked, as I dabbed my forehead with a paper towel for the twentieth time that day.

"I fer sure can be more gloomy, sweetheart. I'm just glad we're all okay. At least I think your mother's okay. Her car is gone, and I assume she made it to work in one piece."

"She did. I called her from school to check on her," Theo said, on his way to the kitchen. He was a total mama's boy, while I was a totally inconsiderate daughter, but my dad never checked on her either, so I wasn't the only douchebag.

I turned on the boob tube, as my dad always called the television set, which confused me as a child. I thought it meant we'd see boobies when the set warmed and produced a picture, but that never happened. I was still baffled why he called it that.

A bang on the front door surprised me. My dad yelled for the banger to come in.

"Everyone good?" It was Chuck. I had forgotten he was around that day but I should've known he was considering he and my dad did everything together.

"We're going to test ride the Miller's 747. You sure you don't want to join us?" my dad asked. I shook my head and focused my attention on the news. A bit of nausea circled my stomach as I felt like a criminal torn between doing the right thing or continuing with my adventure. I absolutely needed something exciting in my life. My dull existence in Sundown reached an expiration date. It was time to dump it down the garbage disposal and hope the drain didn't clog.

"I'll throw dinner in the oven when I get back, ya hear? Y'all be okay?" My dad didn't wait for a reply from me or Theo as he vanished out the door along with his bestie with testes.

Theodore jumped on the sofa next to me and I really wished he wasn't home.

"Don't you have a math book to read?"

"I did my homework at lunch."

"Science? Art? Gym—yeah, gym. Shouldn't you go out and kick a ball around or something?"

"I want to hear about the plane. You don't own this television set, Mamie. They're still down there. The cops and the fire trucks. I saw a news van, too. Life as we know it has forever changed in this split second. Also, I don't know why you're lying about your injuries. You had to have been right there when it happened. I calculated your walking time on the path, and you were literally in the middle of it. You had to be unless you got a ride or went another way."

"Shhh. Here it is." I hushed my brother as the news cast began. He was too smart for his own good, and it really pissed me off. It was his fault I was on the path. I would've been ready for the bus if he hadn't stunk up the bathroom.

"Breaking news. A small commuter plane carrying four passengers and the pilot exploded during descent to Davendale Airport in Sundown this morning at approximately seven-forty-five. No survivors have been found and the cause of the crash is under investigation. The names of the victims are being withheld until families have been notified." The picture cut to a reporter on the scene, smoke billowing from behind. "Missy lives across the street from the crash and saw it happen. Missy, tell us what you saw." Missy was an elderly woman, wearing her pink housecoat with gray, striped cats all over it.

"I seen fyer. I seen smoke."

"What were you doing at the time?"

"I was waiten for Chichi to do number two. She ain't been herself lately and sometimes it's because she ain't had a number two. Constipation can be rough on a poodle and I get it too. Anyway, I looked up and saw the plane. It was wobbly. It was shakin. And then kaboom! It done exploded into a thousand pieces. It looked like that Space Shuttle on the tv."

"You are, of course, referring to the Space Shuttle Challenger disaster earlier this year. Did you see anything else, Missy?"

"Yeah—I saw a girl. I saw a girl running."

"Oh?"

"Yeah. She had a green book bag and she's running like there's ain't gonna be a tomorrow. I guess she was late fer school."

I felt Theo's eyes on me.

"Thank you, Missy. There you have it. The fire in the sky. The tragic plane explosion that took the lives of five people. The names being withheld until families are notified."

I was horrified the old woman saw me, but the reporter didn't seem to care. She didn't ask follow-up questions and quickly ended the segment. It was clear Missy was far from a credible witness.

"I knew it. Now everyone knows it. Why don't you admit it? You can go on the news like that crazy Missy talking about her shitting dog!"

"Yeah, Theo, I should call up the cops right now and tell them I stole something. Tell them I was the girl that weirdo was talking about on the news," I said as I walked to the kitchen to fetch a snack. That news story provided no additional information and it was silly that only the most obnoxious people were interviewed. I was still a bit shaken by my sighting, but something helpful came from it: I realized I needed to be more discreet with the green knapsack.

I searched the cupboards for an open box of Little Debbie snacks while Theo played Atari. I hadn't changed out of the mini skirt and tank top and they still smelled of burnt pine and rubber. Why didn't Devisha tell me I stunk?

"We're eating dinner soon. Dad will be upset with you," Theo said, as I shoved an oatmeal crème pie down my throat. I ignored him and grabbed the phone from the kitchen wall and stretched the cord to my bedroom. The long cord was a new luxury, as that was the only phone in the house and it sucked to have a private conversation when every Blackhead was lounging. The extended cord was a safety hazard, though, but if someone was dumb enough to strangle themselves then so be it.

I called Devisha and we talked about the newscast and the knapsack and the weirdness that the owner had died a horrible death in the sky. Why was a dog collar in the bag and had the canine perished on the plane as well? What else was in the bag? How did the bag survive total annihilation? For once in my life, I was excited to get to school in the morning, but only to investigate the contents of the bag, not because I enjoyed school.

Being dramatic girls, we talked in hushed tones, pretending to be in a Nancy Drew mystery as we devised a plan to get the backpack out of the school safely. I wasn't certain the girl seen running from the accident site was not being investigated.

If only meddling Missy had been focusing more on Chichi's poo instead of exposing me to the world!

CHAPTER FIVE: LORD OF THE WEINER

I scaled the tree to get to the knapsack like a mad monkey, circling each branch with one hand. It was very acrobatic and as smooth as a baby's butt until a branch snapped and I free-fell into an abyss. My stomach rose to my throat, similar to when Devisha took the back roads with her car—pushing her pedal to the metal, over the hills and through the woods but not to grandmother's house. More like a rollercoaster from hell. I looked to the clouds and a small plane appeared. And exploded. I gasped and sat up in my old twin bed, the wooden headboard cracked and dusty. The dream seemed real, as most dreams do when you're able to remember them. If I had to climb the tree again, I wondered if I could do it. Thirty-five years was a bunch of time for a body to weaken and a mind to become rigid and polluted. I had become a creature of habit. I only grocery shopped on Wednesday evenings at seven o'clock. I had five cups of coffee every day—three in the morning and two in the middle of the afternoon. I wondered how anyone got through their days without the energy kick. I was an HGTV junkie. I watched everything from Property Brothers (Jonathan was cuter than Drew) to Love it or List It (the banter was amusing.)

Also, I got in the horrible habit of taking people for granted.

It wasn't intentional and I'd like to think it just happened to everyone. I presumed everyone had family and close friends who became a black heavy bag that hung on a chain in their garages. Punching bags. These bags permanently hung in our homes waiting to be smacked and they had the cracks and rips to prove it. The chains that kept them in place were very strong but I needed to know when to stop punching and when to repair the cracks and rips. I wondered why we mistreated the ones we loved sometimes but pleased strangers on the streets.

I stood from the bed; the knapsack contents still scattered on the faded quilt, as I somehow passed out without rolling onto anything. The morning sun was peeking through the window, beckoning me to start the coffee regimen to wash away the slight hangover. The vintage Mr. Coffee pot still hung from under the kitchen cabinet and I feared it wouldn't work as I pulled a bag of French-vanilla flavored beans from the refrigerator. Coffee and vodka were the only items I packed for this house-cleaning marathon. It seemed my loved ones weren't the only ones I took for granted. I needed to do better with myself.

The coffee brewed slowly, as one would expect from a forty-year-old coffee maker. I was just happy it was dripping at all. I motivated myself before the first sip of momentum and removed the brown trout from the wall to place it somewhere safe. My father's prized catch would live on with Chuck and for that I was delighted. As I moved the heavy dead fish to a cleared corner of the living room, I noticed an engraving on the back of the plank of wood the fish was mounted on.

For Gary: The one that didn't get away, Love Schucker.

My dad's nickname for Chuck was Schucker. It was often used in place of that infamous F word.

Examples included, "Reel it in, you mother Schucker!" or "Awe, Schuck, it was real nice of ya to bring over those fresh tomatoes!" It was funny how they turned Chuck's nickname into an illicit adverb.

Bending to place the hefty fish in the corner, I lost grip and it slipped out of my hands and thumped to the ground, causing a small piece of wood to pop off the mount, just below the engraving. I cursed and bent down to survey the damage. I discovered a small compartment that hid a folded, discolored piece of paper. I pulled it out and carefully unfolded the crispy letter, discovering it was addressed to my dad. I looked at the bottom of the page to see who signed the letter. Not Schucker, but Chuck.

Dear Gary,

I know it's been some time since I shared my feelings for you and even though we've continued to be best buddies, I cannot stop thinking of you as more.

The night we spent together in the truck, broken down in the middle of nowhere was the best night of my life. I realized that night that it was okay to have these feelings, that it was okay to share them with you and it was okay to love another man even when the world thought it disgusting.

I thank you for understanding and opening up to me that your feelings also went deeper, even though you weren't ready to shout it from the rooftops. You aren't ready to act upon or label those feelings and I do not want to pressure you into anything. It is for this reason I have decided to take a teaching position in California. Time and distance will help me reconcile my emotional connection to you. As heartbreaking as this decision has been, I know it is the right one for both of us. I don't want to be held back from finding my true self and I don't want to force you into deciding you may regret.

Just know I will always love you and that anytime I want to feel you next to me I will close my eyes and remember that night in the truck when you placed your hand in mine and told me I was loved.

Love to you always,
Chuck

I sat on my dad's tattered recliner and read the letter again. It was quite eloquent, and this was not the Chuck I remembered. He spoke with a strong southern twang filled with slang. Quite a contrast to the letter. It made perfect sense that Chuck was around often, and my mother welcomed him as part of the family because he didn't have one of his own. He joined us for many dinners, even when my mother was working. He and my dad carried on like an old married couple, in hindsight.

And although my mother sometimes got annoyed at the frequency of his visits, she evidently never suspected he was in love with her husband. The shaking voice and stifled sobs from the elderly Chuck served as confirmation.

He had just found out the love of his life had left *him* this time.

I started crying. I cried that my dad would never sit in the recliner again. I cried because the forbidden love these two men shared lasted two lifetimes but never fully realized. I cried my dad honored his marital commitment even when temptation beckoned. I cried for a lost childhood. I cried for the lack of buttermilk pancakes and maple syrup in the kitchen cabinets. I cried for everything.

"Shut the fuck up!"

Devisha pushed me against my locker door, which was slightly ajar, causing it to slam. Student bodies shot glances.

"Ouch, Dev! What the hell!"

Devisha leaned in and whispered, "Sorry! You were about to get busted with that backpack! I had to create a diversion." It was the day after the commuter plane disappeared from the sky, abandoning the little neon bag, forcing it to take refuge in my school locker. I pulled a fifty-five-gallon trash bag from my back pocket and waited for a couple of stragglers to move down the hallway. The bell rang, indicating we were tardy for our first period classes. Reprimanding wasn't much of a threat considering tomorrow was the last day before a well-deserved summer break.

We quickly transferred the green bag to the black bag. Once it was hidden and the halls cleared, I reached in and pulled out a pair of boy's medium-sized Fruit of the Loom underwear.

"Oh my," Devisha said and snatched them from me. She held them up and inspected for stains. I ripped them away, swatted her and returned them to their home. Next item to see light was Duran Duran's *Rio* on cassette tape. I shared the love of the English band and almost saw their concert in Nashville until my mom grounded me for playing hooky from school. The next deep dive brought a diary or journal to the surface. I handed it to Devisha and shoved the trash bag into my locker.

"It was a boy. That underwear don't lie," Devisha said as I grabbed the journal and hid it under my stack of books and pushed her to move. We said goodbye and split as our classes were in opposite directions. The diary was burning a hole in my hand and I desperately wanted to ditch class and read it but I didn't want to get caught again and grounded from the next Duran Duran concert. Nor would I survive summer school.

"How very nice of you to join us, Ms. Blackhead," my English teacher, Mrs. Weiner, announced as I entered from the back of the classroom. We competed for the most unfortunate last name which depended on which appendage you disliked more: zits or dicks. Zits were the worst. Everyone wanted a dick. Guys were nothing without them and girls wished they had one, or at least the power that having a dick held in the world. Regrettably, feminism was far from alive and well in Sundown.

"Now, ladies and gentlemen, I would like to open the floor for any discussions you would like to have about the tragedy that transpired in our small town yesterday. What kinds of questions do you have?" said Mrs. Weiner, who talked and dressed like a British royal, minus the accent. Her gray hair was the shape of a cantaloupe and she seemed completely out of place in our teeny town. An awkward energy hung over her, like a rain cloud. But she added much needed culture for those of us who cared to absorb her pristine. Addressing us as ladies and gentlemen, though, was a real stretch.

"Did they find any body parts?" Justin asked, bringing gasps and nervous laughs to the Pepto-Bismol colored room. The teacher's mouth dropped and stayed open until she had a response. I was sure the Weiner wasn't expecting to hear that question when she *opened the floor* for discussion. She probably hoped the floor literally opened and swallowed Justin, chewing and spitting the little punk out in chunks. More inappropriateness would follow for decades, but the crazy coincidence of his question was that I knew the answer. To discuss what happened to me on that path yesterday may earn an invitation to the pop group. The IT crowd.

"They found a finger, a torso, arm and a leg," Weiner said.

Justin turned white and lost the smile as the classroom of collective gasps returned. What source was Weiner quoting? It was not reported on the news, and even if bloody parts were found I doubted the habitually happy newscaster Lindsey Rainbow would tell Tennessee.

"If your mother had been on that plane, young man, would you be asking that question? Would you want to know her severed leg, from the kneecap to the ankle, was recovered in a patch of poison ivy? Or that her face was burned to the point of being mistaken for an over-baked pizza?" Another gasp or two from class as well as an *oh my god*. "Let's just talk about the facts. Discussing body parts is the gossip that only comes from people on the scene, and trust me, they aren't talking about that stuff. At least not to children. Let me read you the facts about the victims of this horrific tragedy." Weiner shared new information surfacing overnight. A middle-aged Nashville couple was on the plane, returning from a vacation overseas. The pilot was a resident of a neighboring city. He left behind a wife and a newborn child. Two other passengers, one from Texas, and one from Florida were headed to a Johnny Cash concert just outside of Nashville. They were aged mid-twenties.

Not one of the five victims could fit into boys underwear unless they were extremely small. Someone with dwarfism seemed unlikely. I raised my hand but blurted the question before Weiner motioned to me.

"Wasn't there a kid on the flight? Maybe a teenage boy?"

Mrs. Weiner looked at me, one eyebrow raised. "What makes you ask that, Ms. Blackhead?" I hated when she called me by my last name, my self-esteem was low enough. Fear and regret gripped me as I placed myself under a spotlight in an interrogation room for asking the dumb question. A wave of self-consciousness prompted me to lean forward and placed my elbows on my books, trying to hide the journal that was surely glowing for all the class to see.

"Oh. I just thought I heard someone say that," I said, hoping she quickly replied and moved on to a normal question.

"Who said that, Mamie?"

While I was pleased by my first name usage, I was displeased to devise quick lies. The spotlight was now swinging above my head and I felt many eyes on me, including Justin's.

"I don't know. Someone in the hallway," I said. She quietly stared at me for what seemed like an hour. I didn't look away for fear I would ignite more suspicion as I pulled my stack of books and the journal closer to my chest. I beat Weiner at the staring game and she pulled out a notebook of news she jotted down during Lindsey Sunshine's morning newscast and scrolled.

"I do not recall hearing that. I believe the information I shared was the only information reported. If you know more, please share with the class." She raised her eyes and her eyebrow to me once again.

"I don't. Know more. Nothing." I wished Devisha was in my class. She was the queen of diversion tactics.

After a heavy sigh Weiner finally moved on and pressed the class for further questions. *How did a plane explode in mid-air?* The investigative experts expected it would involve many more months of collecting all the evidence to conclude. *Couldn't parachuting save lives?* Opening the door and jumping right before crashing? The questions skidded off the rails. Too many scenarios in silly action films were referenced as plausible solutions from dying in that plane.

When questions ended and the class quieted, Weiner moved on to the novel, Lord of the Flies, our final reading assignment of the school year; a story with an eerily similar plot—a plane crash and the later discovery of something hanging from a tree. In the book, it was a corpse. I didn't discover a corpse in a tree but the knapsack certainly symbolized a body. As the class began discussing elements of the story, I pulled out the journal and began to read, hoping to learn something about the Lord of the Fruit of the Loom.

Pages one and two were plastered with assorted doodles. Arrows in different shapes and sizes. Trees and circles and squares. No words. Nothing significant yet. I turned to the next two pages. The third was a full-page drawing of skull and crossbones. The fourth page finally had legible words. I began the journey.

September - 1983!

W-WR-WRI-WRIT-WRITE-WRITE! -WRITE!

Doctor or psych guy or whatever his name is told me. I needed to bring something to my next talk with him. I am supposed to write words for how I am feeling so I dont forget.

Okay. How about-I feel tired in the morning because people keep me up all night. I feel grumpy in the afternoon because I'm tired from people keeping me up all night. I feel sleepy in the evening because people kept me up all night.

I pass out at night because I got zero hours of sleep the night before.

But they woke me up again. And repeat.

"How do you feel about his death, Mamie?" Weiner asked, pulling me from my brief visit with the journal. For a moment I thought she was asking about the boy who couldn't get a solid night of sleep. But she was asking about the death of Piggy in Lord of the Flies.

"I was upset. You know, he was a nice boy, and they shouldn't be calling him fat and teasing him because he really tried to be a good leader," I said, throwing a big turd to the wall and hoping it stuck. I hadn't read the book, only the CliffsNotes, like a week ago, and I was bored.

"Simon. Not Piggy. I was asking about Simon's death, Mamie."

I didn't remember Simon. Was he important? Did they cut characters out of footnote versions?

"Also, Piggy wasn't a leader," Weiner said, smugly. I pondered a moment as I squirmed in my chair before creating another poor excuse for an answer.

"I felt bad for Simon. He seemed like a good kid. You know, someone the other boys looked up to. His death definitely affected the others," I said, thinking it sounded decent. Weiner raised her eyebrow again and her hatred for me became obvious. She wished I was in that exploding plane or at least hanging in a tree, dead as a squirrel crossing a freeway. Everything about her expression screamed disgust. I wished she turned her insight to a student who actually cared about the Fly Lord. A kid who enjoyed learning, but I wasn't sure they existed. I wanted to know why the kid in the journal was kept awake. And who kept him awake? I wished this journal was our homework assignment.

"Justin, why do you think Simon had to die?"

"I don't know. Because he was dumb?" Justin was great at comedy and he had a classroom of fans.

"Did anyone complete this reading assignment?" a frustrated Weiner asked as I looked back down at my preferred reading assignment.

Still Sorry Sucky fucky September 1983

Waffles for breakfast again. The darker colored ones that tasted like something burnt. Pouring an entire bottle of syrup on it didn't help. Plus then I get yelled at by the lady of the hour. The one that expects all the kids to bow down to her every word as if she were "royalty". Just because my new home is in the same city as the Royal Highness doesn't mean the workers here are special. This building is rubbish!

Oh- if you want to sound smart, Just put the word royal in front of everything and talk with the accent everyone has here

"Excuse me, but would it be okay if I head to the library for a royal reading session? This building is far from fuckingham Palace. In fact, it is a royal <u>shit hole</u>. Excuse me, madam, but this burnt waffle has given me the royal shits."

See? Sounds so proper.

I came up for air, pretending to be present, listening to the synopsis of the Flies. Mrs. Weiner monopolized the discussion, frustrated with the lack of intelligent debate. Expectations for that assignment should have been extremely low considering kids were more excited about summer vacations and sleeping all day and being as lazy as three-toed sloths.

Laziness didn't register for me. My job started in a few days and a reading assignment solely for me was in my hands with no CliffsNotes version available. The brown leather journal in front of me was as thick as Lord of The Flies and as I fanned the pages I noticed the improvement in the penmanship, which meant the entries scanned years in this boy's life. Separate pages contained poems, or possibly lyrics to songs.

The first poem read:

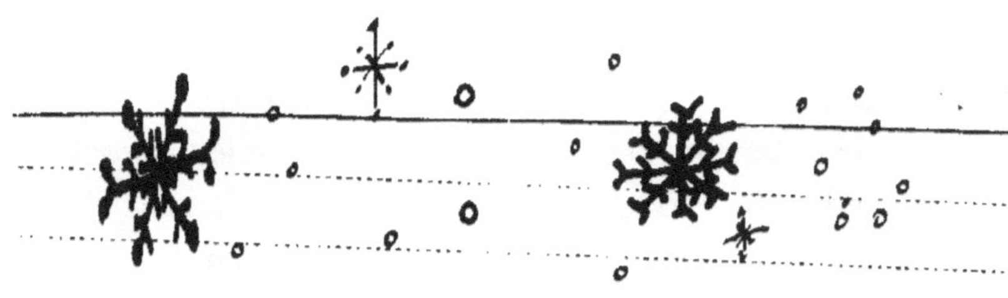

WHITE out. White in. Zig-zagging
through life with the danger or death.
The danger of living.
To live longer and to learn from life
is something not everyone has the
chance to do.
Snow falls and people do too. When
snow falls, it is beautiful, when
people fall, it is tragedy. Paths
are hidden and never found again
in the white.
White out. White in.
Living life in color until the
darkness appears.

Books rarely held my attention but that journal was different. It contained the musings of a person who may no longer be alive; someone who never wanted anyone to read their thoughts, which made me feel like a voyeur. The feeling that a friendship could develop without ever communicating with the author was intriguing yet bizarre.

Did the story of a boy's life end in the passenger seat of an exploding aircraft?

CHAPTER SIX: THE ESCAPE CLUB

Even though my dad progressed to the point of not recognizing his family, I still took comfort in knowing his life force burned like a gigantic candle in the world. His existence was my security blanket, and having that blanket snatched away left me feeling naked in a blizzard. Discovering the deeper love for his best friend was startling, and I wished I could ask him about it. I'm not sure when it happened, but a point in my young life arrived when I was trying to achieve my independence and I stopped learning or caring about the lives of my folks. It wasn't cool to relate to them and their experiences or to discuss their history. I became too stubborn and proud to take their advice or give them the power to decide for me.

First-hand knowledge now proved everyone took secrets to the grave. Mysteries always existed about the people you thought you knew so well, especially triggered when sorting through their remaining physical possessions. Having the power to live in someone's brain for a moment to uncover their mysteries would be my superhero power.

I lived in the brain of the Fruit of the Loom boy. The neon knapsack was his brain and the journal contained his thoughts.

I snuck the over-sized trash bag into the house and rushed to my bedroom where I flung it into the back of my closet and placed an ugly Christmas sweater over it to shield it from view. That sweater taunted me. My dad insisted I wear it the last three Christmases. Frosty the Snowman smiled on the front of the wool pullover, surrounded with extra fluffy cotton and a protruding carrot for a nose. That carrot looked like a penis, and I wasn't sure how it hadn't been ripped off in the washer like the dick of a cheating husband. To make it disappear before next Christmas was my goal for the fall months. A closet fire seemed a great idea.

"Can I see it?" Theo asked, walking towards the closet. For a second I thought he was referring to the sweater and I was ready to grab it by the carrot dick and throw it at him. Then I realized it was the knapsack. That brother of mine always knew too much about me. Another condition of living in a doll house.

"No, Theo!"

"Who did it belong to? Have you figured it out yet?"

"No. I've been in school," I said, making the *der* face.

"Let's look now."

"In a minute. I'm hungry." I started for the door as Theo stood in a trance, looking at the closet. He was just as fascinated with the bag as I was, but this was *my* discovery.

My mystery.

My adventure.

I claimed the knapsack and the secret to unravel and I wouldn't allow him to ruin it for me, but I had to be cool or he would run to my mother and blab and then I'd be grounded. The anticipation and suspense would cease and my summer would be wrecked. I waved him away and followed him out of the room.

Theo and I were the only ones home. Our mother had another late shift, and my dad was still at work— or grabbing a beer with that dirty mother-Schucker. Theo punched a button on the console television and we immediately saw a breaking news story about the plane explosion. The small plane's black box was located and the cause of the detonation would be revealed once the recordings were analyzed and published but it could take months for preliminary results. I wondered if I saw this box and thought it was just a burnt piece of plane as I scrambled from the woods. The newscaster noted that it was rare for a plane to explode in the sky and aviation experts guessed a fuel leak as cause. They once again announced the victims and their ages.

Still no boy.

Maybe the boy wasn't on the plane and the knapsack belonged to one of the adults. Maybe the couple from Nashville had a son who was safely at home and they were returning the bag to him. That theory was weak, how would he be home without them? But if the journal spanned years maybe he was in the states now? Still, I based the idea the bag belonged to a boy because of the underwear. Maybe they weren't boys' underwear, but small man's underwear. I never saw underwear with a *small man* label, though.

"Follow me, Theodore," I walked back to my room and pulled the underwear from the knapsack. "Try these on," I said, handing the tighty-whities to him.

"Umm. No. Weird."

"Okay. I guess you don't want to be involved in any of this, then."

He eyed the briefs and folded his arms, not understanding why I needed him to model a possibly charred boy's used underwear. I told him I needed to confirm that the underwear belonged to someone closer to his age.

He sighed and obliged, taking the underwear to the bathroom. I assumed he would report his findings back to me, but he reentered my room wearing the underwear and nothing else. The vision scarred me for life.

"Are you sure these weren't mine?" he asked, as they fit him perfectly. The owner of the knapsack was a scrawny little nerd as well. He and Theo would've been besties.

"No. Those don't have a landing strip like every one of your underwear do."

"I'm telling mom you're going through my underwear drawer. Gross."

He left the room as I laughed at my quick wit. I investigated the knapsack some more, unzipping the little compartment in the front and removing a toothbrush and an oval-shaped container with a clear teeth protector inside. The squishy, u-shaped plastic protected teeth from grinding. I also had one of these things, but I never used it. Apparently, I moved my mouth around in my sleep like I was chewing on beef jerky, minus the flavor and the meat stuck in every crevice of my dental work. My mouthpiece was also on standby in case I got in a girl fight with a bitchy classmate.

"Why did your brother leave your room in his underwear?"

My dad alarmed me as he appeared in the doorway. I quickly shoved the bag behind me as I violently coughed to distract him, which didn't make sense. A nervous tick, perhaps.

"You scared me! I didn't hear the front door. I don't know why he's running around in his skivvies. He's being a little idiot as always."

Theo returned from the bathroom fully dressed.

"New underwear, kiddo?" my dad asked. I widened my eyes and shook my head when my brother looked to me for an answer. My dad looked at the briefs in his hand and said, "Must be new. No skid marks." He chuckled and walked to the bathroom and closed the door.

"See. Even dad knows. Why can't you wipe your butt like a normal human being?" I asked him.

"Not all humans wipe their butts. The French squirt water up there to clean themselves."

"Yeah, well, we're far from France. Maybe mom can spray some Windex up your butt. She would be happy to do that." Theo nailed me in the face with the briefs. It was a great shot, I must admit. I shoved them back in the bag along with the tooth accessories and removed the journal before hiding the bag back in the closet again as my dad flushed the toilet.

"What is that?"

"Can you give me some space, please. I'll explain later!" Theo was a permanent fixture in my doorway, like a dog begging for table scraps. Much like a dog owner, I'd have to make sure he didn't steal the scraps from the table. I wondered how long I could keep the secret and the bag hidden. Four people knew I had it: Paula, the school nurse, Devisha, Theo, and that nosy neighbor Missy. Missy already told the world, but nobody cared. Paula would keep it to herself because she was a pot dealer. She wouldn't risk exposing a customer's secret for fear her secret would be exposed. I never blackmailed anyone but the thought was intriguing. Devisha was my bestie and I trusted her with my life.

That left Theo, still standing in my doorway, watching me think.

"Leave!"

"Lasagna hittin the oven now. Mom says thirty-five minutes at three-fifty. You won't wanna miss this one. Shur to be the hit of the summer," my dad announced as he walked past my door.

"I'm a make like a tree and leave," Theo said, imitating my dad's twang as he finally left. I stood and kicked the door closed and it slammed harder than I anticipated.

"Leave that sister of yers alone. Ya know she has periods now. When they get those times of the month, they are hard to be around," I heard my dad telling Theo. Just what the door fixture needed to know so he could quiz me about it later. I already heard his drawn-out questions: *"How do you know when it's coming? How long does it last? How do you keep your underwear clean?"* It wasn't my time of the month yet but it was my smoking time of the day. A little buzz was just the unwinding I needed before dinner, plus it brought out the flavor in food. The tangy sausage in the lasagna would have flavor you'd only expect in the finest of restaurants.

I shoved a fan in my window facing outside and slid my new yearbook from the currently ending school year under the door to prevent anyone from pushing it open. This thick book of my pathetic school year replaced a traditional lock on the door handle, since I wasn't allowed to have a door lock. I never understood why. What was I going to do in my room that was so bad besides taking illegal drugs and rummaging through the contents of a stolen neon knapsack? My parents needn't worry about the loss of virginity in my room any time soon because I couldn't get a boy interested in my body to save my life.

I pulled a fresh joint out of a sandwich bag hidden under my mattress and fired it up, sucking in the mind-altering smoke and exhaling a little into the back of the fan, the smoke dancing for a minute outside the window and then disappearing. This was the good stuff that supposedly came from the school nurse's garden. Yeah, I dared her to report me and the stolen bag.

I opened the journal a quarter of the way through to find brown and black smudges all over the open pages. The entry was titled *Escape Club* which further suggested this boy was somewhere he didn't want to be. People kept him awake in the shit hole that served burnt waffles.

I read on after two more power puffs.

October 24, 1983

The plan is set. Me and Adam are busting out of this RUBBISH hole of shit. We can't listen to these stupid people anymore. Yesterday they locked Adam in his room and didn't give him dinner. All because he didn't rake all the leaves from the side yard. They said rules needed to be followed. They said he broke the rules so he needed to be punished. He needed to learn that everyone had responsibilities in life. Everyone had work to do even if they were ten years old. This was not something me and Adam agreed with. We are kids whose family threw them away. Nobody wants us. But we have each other and we can survive out in the world. Adam is the little brother I never had. He is two years younger but we like the same stuff. We both collect bugs and we love playing

Merlin- the electronic wizard game, I
Win at tic-tac-toe everytime. Adam
loves playing Jingle bells on it. We switch
who has it every couple nights. I wish we
could share a room but we cant
because we would be up all night goofing
off. At least that's what the woman in
charge said. We know what we need to
do.   Lady Henshaw orders the
punishments but she should be the one
punished punished for abuse. She needs to
know what it feels like to be hungry all
night, to suffer from bad stomache cramps
Has she ever been hungry a day in
her stupid life? Adam and me have
a joke about her name, Lady Henshaw.
If lady means crack-sniffer, then
she is quite the lady. If not, her name
is a lie. A real lady doesn't act the
way she does. A real lady doesn't
treat people like they shouldn't exist.

Someone pushed at my door but the yearbook only allowed it to open a few inches. I was happy the yearbook was good for something besides serving as a reminder of my tortured youth.

"What are you doing?" It was Theo. Why couldn't he give me two minutes of my own time. He was far from that outstanding little brother-type, Adam, from the journal. "Why does it smell like a skunk in there?"

"Why can't you leave me alone!" I screamed so loud that the closest house, which was half a mile away probably heard. Every time I tried to dive into the journal I was interrupted. I needed to go somewhere quiet and private to concentrate on what I was reading.

The library?

I stayed away from that place like the plague. It was too quiet and depressing. You couldn't even move in your seat without making a noise and it was against the rules to make noise. That suffocating environment was the perfect location for me to read without interruption, though. Located in the center of Sundown five miles from home, I would need a ride if I decided on the house of books and card catalogues.

Sundown Town Center was called the metropolis of the city, but it didn't offer much besides the old library, a few stores and a couple restaurants, including my dad's favorite, Martha's Deli. Corned beef on rye the size of his head was chomped as often as my mom allowed. The two-block center also included City

Hall—the required structure no matter the size of any city for paying taxes and renewing licenses. The closest McDonald's was in the next town. A Big Mac sounded delicious.

"Theodore! What did I tell you about the period!" my dad said outside the door. He was so clueless about the lady-stuff that I had to laugh. It sounded like Theo was being scolded for not finishing a sentence correctly. I rolled my eyes as the door clicked shut.

Theo was a ticking time bomb.

He would explode and I would be grounded for life or something along those lines. If my mother hadn't worked evening shifts this week, he would've spilled the beans already. Their connection was deep and I didn't have the same with her. I'd rather talk to my dad; he was less judgmental and critical of my actions.

The woman who birthed me hated me, or so it seemed most of the time. That appeared a normality as I didn't know any girls who loved shopping and getting nails done or grabbing lunches at Martha's Deli with their mothers to discuss dates and boys and clothes. That was certainly not our relationship. My mother resented my poor sense of fashion and the fact I wasn't a popular girl in school like she was a zillion years ago. She was on the cheerleading team. *I was on the pot smoking team.* She dated a bunch in high school and met several potential husbands. *I met the pillow of my dreams and fell hopelessly asleep, while drooling all over the pillowcase and grinding my bicuspids.* Zero chances existed for me to ever develop into a cool, virgin-less chick. My dad tried to convince me those thoughts were hogwash and I was too sensitive. He also asked if I had received my period yet, like my womanhood drip was a piece of important mail.

Dinner was not yet ready so I opened the journal and continued the journey. I needed to concentrate as my head was spinning—the school nurse's stash was giving me my money's worth. Technically, it was my father's money's worth. Another reason we jived so well; he fed me money anytime I asked, unbeknownst to my mother. He was also the one insisting I get a job at the pool, though, so his funding did have a cease and desist. After the relief of finishing another year of tedious education I would immediately jump into another joyless chunk of day. I almost threw up in my mouth a little thinking about serving nachos and hamburgers and smelling like grease.

My roomate's name is Brandon. He was an accident, as the others teased. His Mother was a lady of the evening. I really wasn't sure what that meant until I asked him one day. Whore. Whats a whore I asked him. A Woman who gets paid to make A man happy. And by happy he didnt mean they cooked them a swanky supper. They got naked for these men. After doing sexy things they got lots of money. But an accident happend. Brandons mom got pregnant and she shot out a baby that grew up to be a shy, rather chunky lug. And then his mom vanished one day and Brandon ended up at Chatterbee Lodge. A home for boys and girls of all shapes and sizes and ages. And problems.

This home was only a real home for ~~the~~ those that believe. But I did like Marie. She was a woman that cleaned my room and asked me questions. Anyway, I want to write that I didn't invite Brandon to join the escape club. I didn't ~~think~~ he could climb into the dumpster. ~~Andzi-That-Banak~~

And I didn't really like him enough to want to spend time in the real world with him. He snored. And farted a bunch and never wanted to get a bath. I did hope he found a home someday. So I guess I care about him a little.

The ESCAPE CLUB Rules:

1. Pack A bag.
2. Don't forget Merlin. ~~Bepsach~~
3. Brush your teeth.
4. Say goodbye in Code so no one knew we will Call this: Hello Sunshine.
5. Sneak to the dumpster after lunch on Thursday before trash pick up.

6. Climb inside and hold your breath.
7. Get dumped into truck and dont Scream.

8. Leave the fenced yard once and for all!!

9. Get out of truck at next Stop.
10. dont let anyone see you.
11. Find A new home
12. BE HAPPY FOREVER

This was our list. We are ready to leave. Once and forever. It is breakfast, Thursday. We are a few hours from the escape. My next page will be all about the escape and our posh new homes.

"Lasagna! Mamie! Dinner!" My dad yelled as the thirty-five minute oven time seemed to fly. Just when the story was getting good. Now I'd sit across the table from my dad and act like I wasn't stoned off my ass while scarfing the sausage and pasta. But first I needed to sneak a peek at the next chapter:

THE ESCAPE
CLUB
TRAGEDY

CHAPTER SEVEN: UNWELCOMING FAMILY

"**Y**ou comin for your mama's best dish ever?"

My father stood on the other side of my bedroom door and spoke just shy of a yell. The door had to be magnetic and each family member had bones of metal because they all stuck to the outside of it regularly and it drove me completely insane.

My stomach rumbled like it understood what was waiting outside the magnetic door but a tragedy was about to happen in the journal. If I didn't continue to read it would be like Dynasty never answering the season six cliffhanger questions. Would Blake Carrington strangle his ex-wife, Alexis? Would the mentally unbalanced Claudia burn to death after a candle ignited curtains in her house? Those fictitious cliffhangers included possible deaths, just like The Escape Club but I didn't have to wait four months until next season for the answers.

"I'm having my period, dad! I don't feel good!"

I saw his eyes widen through the door, like Tom the cat after Jerry the mouse tricks his nose into a mouse trap. I chuckled at the sight.

"Oh, shur. All good. You just come on out when you're feelin better, sweetheart," he said and pulled his metallic body from the door. "See, that's how you handle those awkward lady issues," I heard him telling Theo as he walked back to the dinner table.

"Yeah, but how do you really know it's that time? Couldn't they just tell you that to get out of something?" my brother said and I wanted to kick his ass. He was trying to get me in trouble. The time bomb clock kept ticking and I held my breath, thinking it might explode all over mom's famous lasagna.

"I ain't lookin in the trash can for proof, son. Now get to eatin." *Clinking, clanking of silverware.* I was safe for a moment.

THE ESCAPE CLUB TRAGEDY.
Thursday, October 27th, 1983

We got to the cafeteria at normal time, around 11:45. We stood in line for our lunch of hot dogs that were barly cooked. Seriously, they werent even plump like they were boiled or fried in a pan. It was like they were dumped in a tray right out of the package and thrown on the table. The fries were cold too. How hard was it to make easy lunches in this rubbish dump? It wasnt like there were a lot of kids here. 23 I counted twenty-three a couple days ago. This place was much bigger than the people here. We could have our own room if they would let us. Adam and me sat down and played with our wieners (haha) and fries— making them into dicks and dogs. We talked about how this would be the last lunch we would ever have in this place. We were so excited. And then Rodney sat down next to me !!!! He never sat with us. He was a few years older and wonky and mean. I stayed away from him. (He once broke a little boys pointer finger because he laughed at him for tripping !!!!) He just stared at us back and forth since Adam and me were sitting across from each other.

Back and forth. NO words. I was thinking — what is going on here!!??. Was he going to break one of our fingers too? And then he talked: I'm going with you, he said. I looked at Adam. How did he know about this? only the two of us knew. We swore we wouldn't invite anyone else. Going where? I asked. I was hoping there was a misunderstanding happening — like an episode of Three's Company. (we were allowed to watch the repeat episodes during the daytime.) I'm getting the fuck out of here, he said. You little retards are going to help me or I'll beat the crap out of you, and then I'll tell Henshaw about you. You'll be thrown in the crate for a week

THE CRATE!!!!

In case I turn up dead and someone reads this, (and I always write like someone will read this one day.) It should be fun to read or keep attention anyway. ANYWAY the crate. The crate!!!! Was a crate.

It was a crate made of metal that was in the basement of this dump. It was the size of a refridgerator. Or a coffin. More square, though. You could see out through the gaps when the lights were on but they kept you in the dark most of the time. You couldn't move around much. I only heard about it from other kids. It was bad. If they took you down that hallway – the only way to the basement, you knew you were going to the crate. They fed you because god forbid someone from the higher up visited and found someone skinny from not eating for days they would be in big trouble. They got away with not feeding you a meal here or there above the basement. But the crate was different. They fed you but kept you in the dark. The dark was worse with no food. And there were rats down there. Some of them were able to get in the crate with you and you couldn't get them out without getting bit. Anybody who was down there never wanted to go down there again and would be on their best behavior.

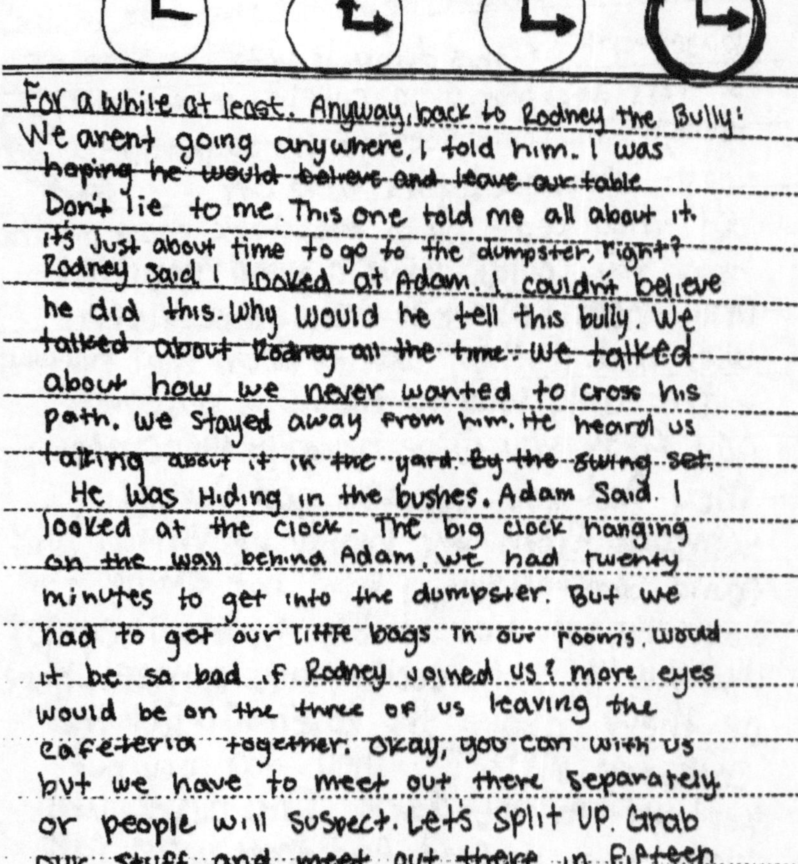

For a while at least. Anyway, back to Rodney the Bully:
We aren't going anywhere, I told him. I was
~~hoping he would believe and leave our table~~
Don't lie to me. This one told me all about it.
It's just about time to go to the dumpster, right?
Rodney said. I looked at Adam. I couldn't believe
he did this. Why would he tell this bully. We
~~talked about Rodney all the time. We talked~~
about how we never wanted to cross his
path. We stayed away from him. He heard us
~~talking about it in the yard by the swing set.~~
    He was hiding in the bushes, Adam said. I
looked at the clock - The big clock hanging
~~on the wall behind Adam.~~ We had twenty
minutes to get into the dumpster. But we
had to get our little bags in our rooms. Would
it be so bad if Rodney joined us? More eyes
would be on the three of us leaving the
cafeteria together. Okay, you can with us
but we have to meet out there separately,
or people will suspect. Let's split up. Grab
our stuff and meet out there in fifteen
minutes. Quarter after twelve is the pick
up time. Rodney the Bully said he didn't need
    to bring anything, which made sense.
Since he always wore the same clothes. He always
smelled like crap. The dumpster would be a
perfect home for him. I said, okay lets
go now. I'll go first. Wait a minute between
the time each of you go after me.

(There were two uniformed workers walking around to keep an eye on everyone-like a prison. This was supposed to be an orphanage - supposed to be a loving home for unwanted kids-not a prison. I couldn't wait to escape.) I walked to the doorway, the only one in and out of the cafeteria. I emptied my tray full of fries and wiener into the trash. I started to walk out the door when I was stopped by one of the workers. Why did you waste all your food? he asked. He was a big man. Tall and wide and I hadn't seen him before. We aren't usually asked this question and I had to think about how I was going to answer. If I said it sucked would I be in trouble? If I said I wasn't feeling good would I be sent to the nurse? Any of these would keep me from getting to the dumpster and my freedom. I wasn't hungry. The food was great though. I said, as I caught Rodney leaving the cafeteria behind me. I watched the big man look at him but not stop him. He said. I nodded and continued to walk out the doorway slowly. I thought maybe he would tell me to stop again but he didn't. I walked fast to the elevator to get to the third floor. We always had to meet outside for yard duty at 12:30 everyday

They took a head count. We were allowed to go back to our rooms before then if we wanted. I made it to the elevator and pushed the up arrow and waited. And waited. Hello Sunshine, I heard behind me. It was our secret code to say goodbye to those we liked. But it was Adam saying it to me. We had a minute to talk about the new member of the Escape Club until the elevator opened. It took a long time for it to come down 3 floors. And it took a long time to go up 3 floors. When it got to floor 3 it beeped but the doors did not open. We pushed the open door open but nothing happened!!!

We pushed the number 2 and number 1 buttons but nothing happened. We were stuck in the elevator. We were stuck in the elevator for an hour. We missed the meeting time. Our escape plan was ruined by a bad elevator. When people realized we were missing and the elevator was broken they came to rescue us. It took another half hour. When the doors opened, Lady Henshaw, the butt sniffer, herself, was standing there. We thought for sure Rodney told on us, thinking we had ditched him. But no, she was there to punish us.

She blamed us for screwing up the elevator. We were locked in our room with no outdoor activity or dinner. We had no idea if Rodney made it out on his own. Later that night, around 7 at night, we were let out of our rooms for a house meeting in the cafeteria. As I walked in I looked for Rodney. I did not see him and guessed he had escaped and that was what the meeting was about. I sat next to Adam but we couldn't talk. The way we looked at each other we could read each other's mind. We both knew this was about Rodney's escape and we were sad we didn't make it out because of that stupid elevator. Lady Butt Sniffer spoke: I'm afraid we have a bit of bad news. One of your housemates thought he would try to leave this facility on his own. He was not chosen by a welcoming family. He was not being picked up by one of his own adult family members. He tried to escape in the trash dumpster. He was ignorant and was crushed dead for it. Please, let this serve as a reminder to not even think about leaving here unless it is with a welcoming family. You will never gain a welcoming family if you do not know how to behave.

We are here to help all of you. The fence
is up with your safety in mind.
We do not want you to suffer a crushing-
I repeat- a CRUSHING fate like the
one that befell the dear child, your friend,
Rodney. Lady BS kept talking about
respect and manners and cooperation
but I zoned out as I imagined what
it must have felt like to have the snot
smashed out of you. I thought about
what a stupid plan it was. About how
even though we knew that truck
crushed trash, we didn't think it
crushed live boys. We were so dumb.
And Rodney paid the price. I was thankful
for the broken elevator but also felt
bad. Even though Rodney was never a
member of the Escape Club, it was our
plan that killed him.

I closed the journal and rested my head on my pillow as I absorbed the story. If Fruit of the Loom boy was twelve in 1983, he would be fifteen now, the same age as me. That meant in three years from that journal entry he'd meet his maker while flying in Tennessee. Possibly. The thought that his life may have ended above my head gave me the heebie-jeebies.

Lasagna. My stomach wanted to escape through my mouth and beat me to a pulp for ignoring its hunger.

"It's about dang time," Theo said as I sat at the table with the chipped wood on the corner. I ignored his comment, thankful he was alive and dorky. He and my dad cleaned up the sauce on their plates with garlic bread as the phone rang. Theo rushed to answer and handed the butter-slimed receiver to me. I swallowed a forkful of noodles as Devisha said:

"Guess what we're doing tomorrow night, girl thang?"

"Rejoicing school is over?"

"Actually, yes. We were invited to Justin Whitney's party. Shhh, it's on the down-low. His parents are out of town." I carried my meal into the bedroom, dragging the cord behind me. My dad tried to protest but abruptly stopped as he remembered I was having my fake period. He wouldn't fight with me about eating in my bedroom that evening.

"Are you kidding me? Why? Those people hate us!"

"Well, this is your doing, actually. Apparently, Tanya Spencer took a liking to you and asked Rachel Yeardly to invite me and you. We're in, baby! We have made it to the big leagues and we're going to rock the shit out of that Whitney house!"

I shoved the fattest lasagna noodle ever into my quivering mouth and chomped with such ferocity I was sure my tongue was amputated.

"This is great, right? Aren't you pumped?"

I shoved another forkful of meat and sauce into my mouth, giving new meaning to stress eating. I wasn't sure how to respond and keeping my mouth full delayed an answer. Why the party invite from the girl who caught me in multiple lies? I was convinced it was a ploy to humiliate me. No other explanation existed.

"Girl, you're sounding like a pig burying its nose in a steaming pile of shit. What the hell are you doing right now?"

When I swallowed the last chunk of sausage, I shared my suspicions that we might end up like Carrie at the prom in that horror movie, only covered in hot sauce instead of pig's blood. She questioned the hot sauce; told me I was dumb and firmly suggested I put together an outfit for the party of the year and then hung up before I chewed the second largest noodle ever.

The next entry in the journal was a poem:

SINGLE UNCLES FOR A REASON

IF NOBODY ELSE IS THERE IT WAS PROBABLY A BLOODY SEASON

WHEN DAY AND NIGHT BRINGS CONFUSION AND FEAR

LIGHT AND DARK WILL NEVER STOP A TEAR

LOOKING FOR STRENGTH AND A FIGURE TO TAKE CARE OF ME

IS LIKE ASKING FOR COMFORT AND LOVE FROM A MAPLE TREE

MICROWAVES ARE SUPPOSED TO WARM MY BELLY

BUT END UP EXPLORING A POOR FURRY SAP NAMED KELLY

Poems were nonsensical to me. The interpretation aspect was puzzling. I tucked the journal under the bed, swallowed the last of the lasagna and headed for the closet as my stomach quieted and thanked me with a belch. Preparing for the social event of the summer would distract me from reading for a bit and I had to overcome my anxiety and figure out how to not look like a Monchhichi. But I still needed to be *oh so soft and cuddly.*

My social status was going to transform in a big way.

CHAPTER EIGHT: DANCE OF THE DEAD

Deciding what to keep and what to throw in the dumpster was difficult. Memories distracted me and they surfaced easily since nothing changed after I moved out at nineteen. It was effortless for my mind to revisit a return home from an awful day of school or stress that the clothing hanging in my closet wasn't cool enough. (Spoiler alert—it wasn't!) My mother always kept the refrigerator stocked, so the currently empty icebox jerked me back to the present and forced me out of the house to visit the old town circle for nourishment.

The buildings downtown looked mostly the same and City Hall hadn't changed at all. Martha's Deli was sold and renamed at least five times over the years, but currently deserted, with boards covering windows the neighborhood hooligans smashed with rocks. I found a coffee shop that served a few food items beating out my next option of gas station pizza or BBQ chips. I grabbed my coffee and a window table and anxiously awaited my tuna on toasted rye. My right hand trembled from lack of solid food and an overdose of caffeine as I stared out the window at the closed movie theater across the street, recalling the fun I had sneaking back and forth from the two screens it housed. Two hit movies for the price of one ticket. It was scandalous back in the day and I felt like a rebel seeing Annie and ET in the summer of eighty-two, multiple times each. My dad dropped Theo and me off in the morning and returned for us in the afternoon. He used the theater as a babysitter and wasn't concerned about the kidnapping threat as it was rare in our little town. We did things growing up that aren't done anymore, like walk a mile to the store by ourselves, play in the streets bare footed after a hard rain, and talk to strangers. We talked face to face with friends and family and shared intimate details of the day, live and in person; we didn't share on a social media website on a tiny computer screen disguised as a phone.

A text notification vibrated and I pulled my tiny computer screen disguised as a phone from my purse. My fifty-year old eyes couldn't see without reading glasses so I had to dig those out of my purse as well.

Abigail was at the house and wondering what happened to me so I punched my whereabouts into the phone and continued to stare out the window, my eyes catching a clothing boutique. The space used to be a thrift store that stocked gently used clothing and was the spot I got new hand-me-downs for each school year. It was there I found the outfit for the party at my future husband's house. The anticipation leading up to that party was ulcer-inducing for I had the potential to be a popular girl but I needed to prove my worth. My stomach soured as PTSD gripped my body and held my hand as I journeyed back to that time. The party and my performance did make me popular the following school year.

For all the wrong reasons.

Devisha pulled me into the thrift store named *Newman's Garb*. Most people referred to the shop as *Newman's Garbage*. The popular girls wouldn't step foot inside and teased those who did. Bitches. I couldn't wait to become one, but first I had to survive the shopping trip. It was Friday, the last day of the school year, and we were dismissed early so the teachers could consume crazy amounts of liquor and gossip about the worst students of the year.

"Look at this! Classy!" Devisha held up a multi-colored jean jacket. Blue and black with two big chest pockets. It was okay, but way too big for me. I smiled and nodded and walked a few steps to the women's shirt section, organized by color. Lots of hideous greens and blues with stains or discolorations from countless washings. Success was usually achieved in the men's section, so I skipped to those racks to find acceptable threads.

"This shit has to be better than acceptable. It has to be phenomenal!" Devisha said when we first walked in the door, pushing me to adjust my expectations. I grabbed a multi-colored plaid flannel and held it up. "Don't even think about it, girl thang. You'll be swimming in that. You want to accentuate your curves. Small and tight."

"But I'm flat."

"We'll put a little cushion in there."

"With what?"

"Cushion! I'll rip up one of those patio cushions on our back porch. No one will miss it, trust me."

I was a dumbass and trusted her. More on that later.

Looking through the small shirt sizes I settled on a Mickey Mouse t-shirt with a lipstick stain on the white collar, clearly a girl's shirt hiding in the men's section. It was cute and I'd fill in the entire collar with red marker to mask the stain. Devisha was not convinced the selection screamed phenomenal, but I sold it by suggesting we accentuate Mickey's eyes with boob cushion and accentuate my ass with a tight pair of jeans. Fully displaying my girl parts made the outfit phenomenal.

Madonna echoed over the loud speaker and inspired me to search the table of random clothing items for something to pull my brown, shoulder-length hair back, just like the queen of pop. I found a white, cotton belt formerly part of a bathrobe. Devisha worried the look could provoke our classmates to sing *Like a Virgin*. The lyrics would be wrong for me, though. I wasn't like a virgin; I was a virgin. Probably the only virgin left in my school, except for Janet Williams. She supported abstinence and screamed it from the school rooftops, probably settling into a nun's habit someday and only being touched by a man spiritually.

Devisha thrusted her hips as she danced to the song. She bent over and pretended to get plowed from behind and sold it well, having just tried it a couple months ago with her boyfriend. She moaned realistically, too. I laughed and looked to be sure no one was watching, spotting two people approaching the double glass doors. I motioned for Devisha to stop the plowing as the entrance door swung open and a classmate and her mother entered.

It was Tanya.

She was one of the girls who blacklisted others for shopping at the thrift store. Tanya—the popular girl who invited us to the swankiest high school party of the year.

To see her at Newman's Garbage was shocking and terrifying. I quickly pulled Devisha to her knees behind a circular rack of smelly coats and jackets to hide. Miss Popular walked past us on the other side of the stenchy rack and continued to the formal-wear section as we raised our heads and spied. Her mother, the nurse that Tanya may or may not aspire to be when she grew up, grabbed a shiny, sequined dress, and held it up. Tanya looked at her mom like she was an idiot and swatted the awards ceremony costume away and pulled a puffy, green gown off the rack and held it against her body. It was too dressy for a house party but acceptable for a prom or a tea party at Mrs. Weiner's house.

"I love that! I want it!" Devisha said.

"No! It's too dressy," I said, rolling my eyes.

"Bitch better not take it. It's phenomenal."

"Oh my god. You've said the word phenomenal like twelve times in the last ten minutes. You do remember we're in a thrift store, right? All of these clothes are worn and have pit stains." Tanya took the phenomenal dress and a couple mediocre dresses to the changing room. We only hid from her mother now.

"What are you girls doing?" A large bald man wearing a manager badge appeared from nowhere, scaring the bejesus out of us. "We do have security cameras all around. Don't think about stealing anything or the cops will be here like white on rice." I didn't know if the older authority figure made a racial slur or if he was simply the un-coolest thrift store owner ever to exist.

Squatting wasn't the best idea and proved suspect and we cautiously stood with our backs to Tanya's mother.

"Oh, no. we're not stealing, sir. I lost my necklace. Please keep an eye out for it. It's a leather shoestring with the skull of a white person on it. You know, like a charm. The skull is white."

Devisha made that up on the fly, not the first time she concocted a story without notice. Also, it seemed she took the *white on rice* comment as racist, and that wasn't the only instance of discrimination. Many times during our friendship people glared at her like she was a monster or stepped away from her if she got too close. In competitive sports at school, she was called that dreaded N-word when she kicked some white girl ass during kickball or basketball. I was called an N-lover multiple times just for hanging out with a girl as dark as a Hershey's bar.

The store guy shook his head and walked away. I turned to be sure Tanya's mother hadn't spotted us, but she was gone; probably in the dressing room telling her daughter she was beautiful and trying to convince her to become a nurse so she could one-up her husband. The power play for Tanya's future was happening in the changing room of the filthiest thrift store in Tennessee. To expose Tanya for garbage shopping would be a taste of her own medicine but my shot at popularity would be destroyed.

I convinced Dev the one-piece jumper she wrapped around her waist was phenomenal and hurried her to the cash register. I wouldn't be caught dead in an adult onesie but we needed to escape before we were discovered and uninvited to the party.

The man who suspected us thieves rang up our selections as he stared at our bodies, looking for a protruding shoe in a pocket or a trinket from the aisle of useless home décor stashed in our bras. We paid and fled and talked about Tanya on the way home, wondering why she shopped at a thrift store when her parents were professional millionaires. Had she pulled a Mamie and lied about their careers?

After cutting through some neighborhood lawns, we arrived at my house to find Theodore and his friend Charlie playing Super Mario Brothers. With my mom working and my dad missing yet again we headed straight to my room to avoid interaction with my brother's friend who annoyed me to the max. Devisha pulled out the knapsack and lit a joint. I caught her up to speed on the boy living in an orphanage and how the bully kid was crushed while trying to escape. She thought it was wild and opened the journal to the next page.

The house of misfit children was holding a dance.

A mixer for all boys and girls.

Much like the party I was attending in a few hours. Minus the booze

THE DANCE OF THE DEAD
November 12th, 1983

It has been weeks since Rodney was killed. I couldn't write anything more until now. I was dry. In shock. The mood of Chatterbee Lodge was bad. Quiet. I think the kids thought the only way out was to die. The only way we would ever leave this pokey was to die because nobody would ever rescue us. Nobody wanted the trash of London. The metro police stopped in to ask questions but they didn't stay long once they decided his death was an accident and that he was trying to escape. It was his own dumb fault. Me and Adam kept our lips sealed. The last we needed was Henshaw finding out we were planning to escape (get crushed) as well. We would've been in the crate for a week. The thought scared me.

I had never been down to the basement but I heard enough stories. To liven up the place and to change the mood, Henshaw announced we would have a dance. They were allowing all boys and girls to come togther. Most of the time they kept boys and girls apart. The girls stayed on the first floor and the boys stayed on the second and third floors. We were allowed to eat meals together but couldn't play together. That doesnt mean it never happened. And the really bad girls would visit the crate too. They didnt have a less scary form of punishment. There were only five girls here right now. The girls never stayed long. Couples always wanted girls before boys. Boys had bad reputations. I always thought it was funny when the rotten girls found a welcoming family. I always thought about what the family had in store for them once they got to know the real girl - not the fake one putting on a show...so they could get out of Chatterbee. A few times girls were returned. I always got a chuckle out of that. It did force them to change if they ever wanted back out.

ANYWAY - Let's Dance!

I met the girl of my dreams at the dance. Is it possible to fall in love at age twelve? And how hadn't I seen Ruby before? She had been there for a couple days. She was twelve, too! She had long red hair and blue eyes. I never really paid attention to eye color before but hers almost glowed. I couldn't look away from them. Adam punched me to snap me out of a trance

When we met her. She was shy. She looked down after the punch, like she knew I was in love with her. The four other girls led her away after that. They took her away from me. They were all younger. I'd say ten and under. Ruby would act as their big sister. I had seen it before with older girls. They became almost like the mother. of the girls. I had no idea how long Ruby would be at Chatterbee. I had to make my move fast. She was the bee's knees. Are you bloody serious? Adam asked me and then punched me again because I was still staring at her walking away. I was still in a trance.

I asked Adam for his help. I needed to dance with her.

He made me sit down with him to take it all in. Don't get attached, Martin! he told me I didn't care if she was going to be adopted tomorrow, I wanted to spend as much time with her as

I could. The dance was in the cafeteria. Tables were moved to make a dance floor in the middle of the cafeteria. Everyone sat around, not wanting to be the first to go out to dance. Ruby sat across the empty dance floor from me and we made eye contact three times. Each time she would look away and put her head down. She was the shyest girl ever! And she seemed very sweet. She would have a welcoming family in no time. I knew I needed to act fast, so I made Adam go talk to her. I watched him yell in her ear because the song Der Kommissar was blasting. She looked over at me and this time she didnt look right away.

She actually smiled at me. A big smile. And I saw crooked teeth. Not just a gap, or one crooked tooth, but her whole front teeth looked like she was beaten with a lead pipe until they twisted and turned. This time I looked away and then down to the ground but not because I was shy but because I wasn't sure if I wanted to dance with her then. I thought she could really hurt my lips if we kissed. How was it she didn't hurt her own lips when she talked? Adam came back she would love to get down with you. Like really. I asked Adam if he saw her fangs. He said who gives a shit. Shes a girl who needs a man. Be her bloody man. I looked across the room at her again and she was smiling big. Oh — my — god! I had never kissed a girl but I knew there was tongue involved. I thought about the pain that could happen. And then a slow song started playing and she stood and motioned for me. She was suddenly not shy anymore.

WE DANCED !!!

I don't know if it was smooth or messy. Adam said it looked okay. We were the only ones out there and I could see everyone staring. At one point Lady Henshaw came out and pulled us away from each other. I wasn't the one getting closer. Ruby was. It was like she was trying to get fresh with me. She seemed to breathe faster and some of her breath blew into my ear. I felt something below. I had started what we were taught at Chatterbee was puberty. I had hair and I got boners. I knew what sex was from the other boys but I didn't think you were allowed to do sex until you were a grown up. AND THEN SHE KISSED ME!!! I wasn't ready for it. She put her whole mouth over mine and shoved her tounge inside my mouth. I gagged when her tounge hit the back of my throat. I didn't know tongues were that long. I knew lizards had long tongues but not people. Henshaw ran out and grabbed Ruby and pushed me away! I almost fell on my butt! The dance is over!

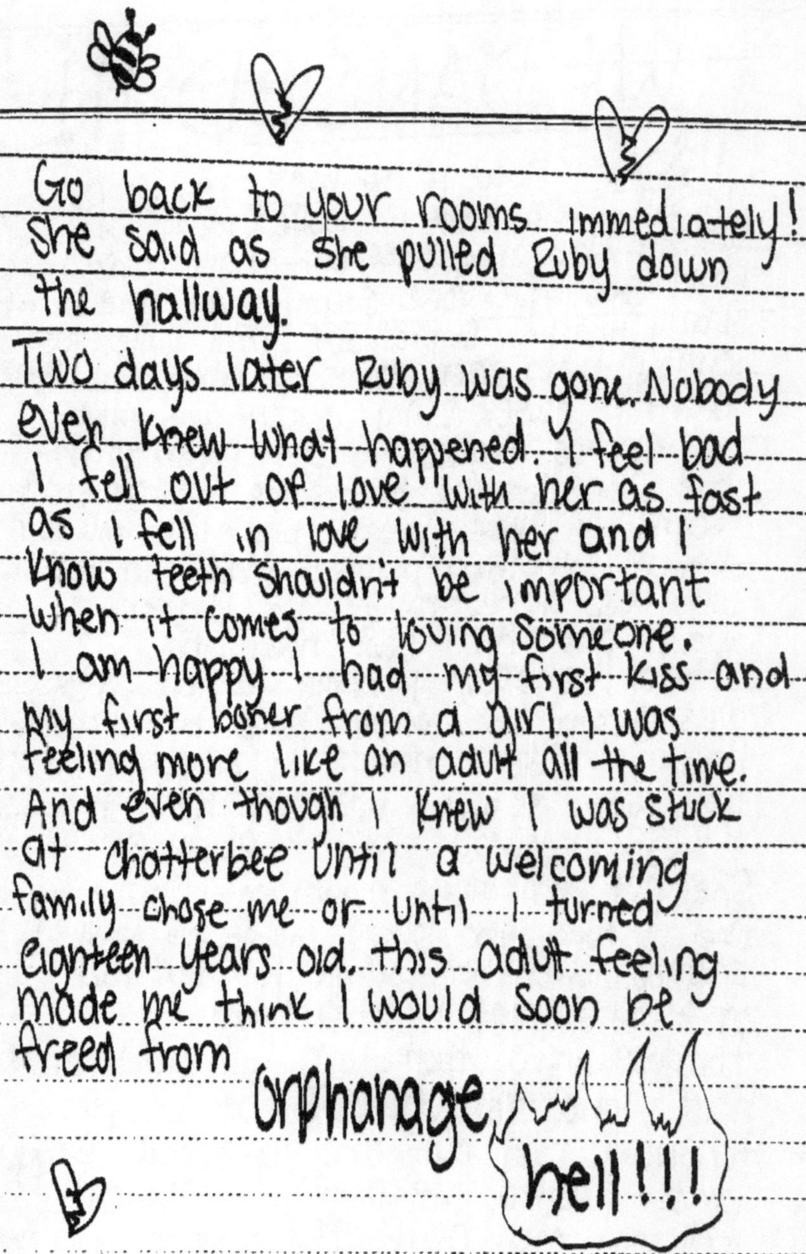

Go back to your rooms immediately! She said as she pulled Ruby down the hallway.

Two days later Ruby was gone. Nobody even knew what happened. I feel bad I fell out of love with her as fast as I fell in love with her and I know teeth shouldn't be important when it comes to loving someone. I am happy I had my first kiss and my first boner from a girl. I was feeling more like an adult all the time. And even though I knew I was stuck at Chatterbee until a welcoming family chose me or until I turned eighteen years old, this adult feeling made me think I would soon be freed from orphanage, hell!!!

"Martin! His name is Martin!" I was happy to finally stop calling him the Fruit of the Loom boy.

"Martin got him some wood," Devisha exclaimed and laughed. "I wonder if he gets laid at all in this journal." She skimmed some pages. "Do you think you'll beat him to the punch?" she asked me and I shrugged as I fantasized about inventing a boy I met at the movie theater over the summer. This boy and I had a scorching love affair while he visited from California and I allowed him to touch me after shoving a handful of popcorn into his mouth. My nickname of the new school year: *Butter Crotch*.

"Are you getting high in there," a voice from the other side of the door asked. It was Charlie, and I was surprised it took that long for him to be annoying.

"Don't you have a Mario Bro to play with? And by Mario Bro, I mean your little baby dick," Devisha yelled and started cackling. I found it amusing, too. The thought of Charlie playing with his nearly non-existent penis was hysterical.

"Lamie Mamie put me to shamie," Theo repeated loudly about ten times to get back at me for laughing at his buddy.

A car honk ended the taunting, signaling our ride was outside to take us to Devisha's to prep for our coming out debut. We were debutantes in a world that only existed in our minds. I hid the knapsack in the back of my closet again and covered it with the same ugly Christmas sweater. I asked Frosty the Snowman to watch after Martin and Adam and if the journal was a Disney story, Lady Henshaw was the evil queen and could suck a fat one.

I told Theo not to step foot in my room and he warned me not to leave the house until dad got home. My dad never insisted on that before, but I had never gone to a high school party and he was concerned I'd get plastered. I swore I wouldn't drink, which was stupid since I did substances much worse in my bedroom, and those illegal drugs were given to me by a woman from his high school who he supposedly boinked before dating my mom.

About an hour later I was in Devisha's bedroom and I looked like Raggedy Ann, proving I had absolutely no clue how to apply make-up. Dev wiped me clean and tried again, giving me colorful eye shadow and bright red lips. After a light powdering on my cheeks, we mutilated the family's outdoor furniture and over-stuffed my bra with smelly foam. Mickey Mouse's eyeballs were about to blow from their sockets.

"Don't you think it's a little much?" I asked Devisha. "People will know I'm packing."

"They'll know you're packing, alright. Packing love, baby. You are the real deal. You are a hot bitch!" We stood side by side in the full-length mirror that leaned against her bedroom wall. She was three inches taller and five inches thicker. Her onesie outfit grew on me but I would never want it on me, it was still ugly as sin, but if anyone could rock the look it was my bestie. And with my hair tied up exposing my revised layer of make-up, I felt pretty.

"Are y'all gonna just stand there all night? That face won't last forever, ya know," Devisha's mom said from the doorway. Minutes later we sat in the backseat of the family station wagon and I tried not to vomit as reckless driving combined with a nervous tummy threatened to destroy my evening. I closed my eyes and saw Tanya in that ugly gown and that comforted my anxiety until my eyes opened and I saw my enormous fake boobs and wanted to vomit again.

The wagon literally squealed to a stop; the brakes so worn that I suspected Devisha's mom would fly off a cliff on the way home.

"You sure this is the right address? Ain't no one here," Devisha's mom said, and she was right. No cars in the driveway and only one light shined from a window. Devisha checked the handwritten address and nodded. She asked her mom to wait until we got inside and out of the wagon we ventured, hearing no signs of a party gone out of bounds. The door flew open a second after we rang and Devisha's friend, Rachel, greeted us with squeals and hugs. We waved to Dev's mom and the vision of her big, screaming face as the wagon flew off a winding road made me chuckle. Once inside, the floor vibrated under our feet as jamming was going on in Justin's basement, which made sense since it was a secret party. Parking was down the street as to not alert the neighbors. We took the stairs down to the large ground floor and I was relieved that the music was loud and the lighting was dimmed; it felt safer, like no judging happened if you weren't seen in your entirety. Also, I could hide in any corner if necessary. Devisha and I blended with the other hot bitches in tight clothing. It looked packed but no elbowing was needed to get through the crowd.

"You made it!" I heard and turned for the answer to Tanya's wardrobe choice. She wore the obnoxious, green prom gown, only she made some alterations. She cut a "V" in the front to provide a launching pad for her boobs, removed the sleeves and shortened the length. I had to admit both the restyled dress and Tanya looked amazing. She wrapped her arms around me and our boobs pressed against each other's as I welcomed the embrace of popularity. Fake boobs fit the scene of fake people, and that also helped my anxiety. My entire sense of self changed in a couple days starting with my heroics at the exploding plane scene and then Tanya and I stooped to each other's levels—she at my thrift store and I at her party. The connection was real, but I had to know:

"You look great. Where'd you get the dress?"

"Thank you! My mom took me into Nashville and we found a cute little shop."

Tanya kept it as real as my chest and I wondered if that was the basis for popularity. Did clique members really care for each other and did they confess truths? I couldn't drop my guard and the fear of a public humiliation returned.

"Stop cheating on me!" Justin teased as he witnessed Tanya hugging me a moment earlier. "Can I have some of that?" he asked his girlfriend and then wrapped his arms around me. Another chest squeeze, much tighter than Tanya's, and I caught a whiff of the moldy cushion foam. I think he smelled it too, as he quickly released me and skipped away like the cat that ate the canary.

"Let's hit the bar!" Tanya said, trying to pull me away from Devisha, but I grabbed my bestie's hand and dragged her along. The bottles of booze were lit from behind and projected beautiful shades of blues and yellows and reds onto the basement ceiling. I lacked experience with booze, only ever trying vodka once and it sucked. Devisha was drunk multiple times and told me it differed from a pot buzz.

"What can I pour you lovely ladies?" a very cute boy behind the bar asked us and I almost replied, *I'll drink anything you want to pour down my throat*. I was in love, much like Martin and the redhead at the orphanage; I only hoped the bartender had a better smile.

"We'll take a shot of that one," Tanya pointed to a bottle of brown liquid and the stud poured two shots. The little sippy glasses seemed safe; the amount of booze wouldn't knock me out. We cheered and I took a sip, the liquid immediately burning a trail to the organ that was about to vomit just minutes ago. "Drink it all at once!" Tanya yelled over the song *We Don't Have to Take Our Clothes Off to Have a Good Time,* and I guessed the lyrics didn't apply to anyone in the basement. She finished her drink with one gulp and I did the same. Our friendship couldn't begin with me being a pussy-face. I screamed and laughed and then saw Devisha not screaming or laughing, having been excluded from the first shot.

"Yeah. Looked good. Why don't you get drunk with your new best friend and I'll find someone else to hang out with," Devisha said, and then disappeared into a cloud of smoke. I called after her and stepped away to follow but Tanya grabbed my arm. She asked if I liked the drink and if I wanted another. She also introduced me to Byron, the adorable bartender and my eyes turned to huge, red, pumping hearts and I think I drooled. *Girls shouldn't act like that;* I heard my mother saying. *Girls never make the first move; girls shouldn't be easy or they'll get a bad reputation. You don't want a bad reputation, do you, Mamie Blackhead?*

Byron was a good friend of Justin's from a neighboring city and he was an experienced bartender at the ripe age of sixteen, but he needed my help as the demand for spirits was strong, so I slithered behind the bar like a sexy snake with fake patio cushion tits and helped him pour shots. The action kept me from drinking too much.

Thirty minutes later I followed him up the stairs to the bathroom.

Devisha went cold, both emotionally and physically; I didn't spot her anywhere. The basement was a disgusting haze of cigarette smoke and pot smoke and I was sure she was still down there somewhere, but it was okay if we weren't attached to each other all night. I planned to locate her after my bathroom break with the first boy I ever loved.

"Hey, now we can actually hear each other," Byron said as we reached the hallway, the basement music now just background noise.

"What? Did you say something?" I joked, my ears still ringing from whatever country song was blasting. It was musical tug of war, from pop to country to new-wave and alternative. I cringed when country won the tugging match. My mouth still tasted of cinnamon candy and gasoline, the four shots marinading in a non-tubular way. I felt tipsy, I guessed, but I had my senses about me and I wasn't about to fall on my face or anything, and if Byron tried to kiss me, my breath was acceptable. Gas and cinnamon prevented gingivitis.

"You're really pretty, you know that? Can I kiss you?"

Had he read my mind? Was he some kind of psychic, mind-reading, Tom Cruise wannabe? He certainly reminded me of the actor, both in looks and swagger, and I needed to decide if I should pucker at his first request or if I should play *hard to get*, as my mother nagged. I thought of my limited kissing experience, my cousin being the most serious, when I was ten. Kissing cousins sounded gross, but our tongues didn't touch and he wasn't my first cousin, so it seemed acceptable. I was totally destroying the moment thinking about my second or possibly third cousin with the bushy eyebrows.

"It's okay. There's a bathroom around the corner and there is one upstairs. You take the one down here and I'll run upstairs," he said and I heard a game show buzzer, the sound of a losing contestant. I worried my pause changed his mind about kissing me and he'd move on to find another set of lips.

I wanted to win the showcase showdown.

When he turned and started for the stairs, I grabbed his hand and yanked him around. I didn't mean to yank so hard, but he quickly spun and I went in for the kiss, which meant I had to stand on my tippy toes. Our lips touched and he tripped over his feet and pulled me to the floor next to him. It was awkward and embarrassing, but we giggled for a moment and then he mounted me, kissing my cinnamon lips as we started making out on the floor of the hallway. Our tongues did that thing Devisha called *tonsil tag*.

"Get a room!"

Justin stood above us, like a paramedic ready to resuscitate an unconscious heart attack victim.

"And I don't mean my room. Stay the hell out of there. My sheets were just washed, you sickos," he warned as he stepped over us to enter the downstairs bathroom. Byron smiled and kissed me again before pulling me to my feet.

"I guess we're both headed upstairs," he took my hand and led me up the stairs. I admired his plaid shorts, squeezing his slender butt. He had a very fit body and the polo shirt helped to promote his toned chest. I imagined he was following the orders of a desk clerk in a sleazy hotel and leading us to a room with cockroaches and bed bugs. He playfully pushed me in the bathroom and closed the door, waiting his turn in the hallway. I passed the mirror and screamed. My left fake boob had dropped. It looked like Mickey was punched in the eye and his bottom lid had swollen. I adjusted the grody foam and realized I couldn't get a room with Byron. He'd discover my fake, moldy boobs.

I removed the stuffing from my bra and flushed it down the toilet. It took about five suicidal flushes to kill it all, but the delay allowed me to freshen my chest and re-stuff my bra with tissues, just enough to plump my chest a bit. Tissues were acceptable and didn't reek of two-day-old forgotten clothes in a washer.

"You okay in there?" Byron asked as I finished my return to normality and rushed out the door, brushing against him as he rushed in the door. I waited in the hall until my bladder kicked me solid and I realized I never peed! I hurried downstairs to the toilet, hoping to get back upstairs before Byron finished, which was probably the dumbest thought of all time. Boys just whipped it out and peed everywhere and shoved it back in, their dribbles soaked up by their underwear.

I shoved the restroom door open to find Justin sitting on the toilet.

"Ummm. Rude."

I gasped and closed the door and after a few deep breaths I yelled through the door, "You know those little round buttons in the middle of the door handle? Those are called locks."

"Can you come in here. I need some help."

"What?"

"I ran out of toilet paper. It's under the sink and I can't reach it."

What were the odds I would be at a party with a hot guy in each bathroom wanting my attention either out of necessity or attraction?

"Come on. I flushed the disgusting odor away."

He wasn't lying. The bathroom didn't smell like the one at my house after Theo unloaded. I pushed the door open and held my hands over my eyes, peeking through to follow Justin's pointing finger to the cabinet under the sink. I found bath salts and towels and three dispensers of cream-colored hand soap.

"No toilet paper in here," I said, panicked to be in the same room with a half-naked boy from the football team. The most popular boy in high school, exposed for me to see if I turned my head slightly to the right.

"Yeah, there is, keep looking."

I dug behind the towels, but no Charmin; I assumed this family stocked only the best paper for their behinds, considering they had the funds to vacation in the Bahamas while Justin destroyed the house.

"Try the cabinet on the other side. And please close the door. This is embarrassing enough. And by embarrassing, I mean em-BARE ASS-ing!" Justin chuckled and then sighed. He was weirder than I imagined for a popular football player. I opened the narrow floor-to-ceiling closet and saw more towels, a bunch of medicines and ointments, and a couple double-packs of Kleenex, but again, no toilet paper.

"Here you go," I handed him a tube of Preparation H and chuckled.

"Funny! If I sit here any longer, I'll need that shit."

"Okay. Seriously. Did your mom forget to stock you up before she left?"

"Just give me a towel."

"Ew. Gross."

"Look, at this point it dried up down there. Like dirt. It won't be a smooth wipe by any means. Just wet the towel and hand it to me and you are free," Justin said, as I wondered what colored towel would be best. I grabbed a navy-blue one and ran it under the stream of sink water. "I hope that's warm water," he warned, and I turned the cold off and ran the hot until it was just starting to get warm.

"You look great tonight, by the way."

My face reddened and steam rose from my head. A second boy was complimentary and I wanted to freak out. "Thank you," I said and squeezed the excess warm water from the towel that was about to swipe his dirty butt. I kind of wanted to wipe him, to have him lying on his back with his legs in the air.

"Any day now," he said.

My weird, trance-like smile faded and I stopped fantasizing about wiping his baby butt and handed him the towel instead. I accidentally glanced at his pubic hair and possibly the base of his penis.

"I'm glad you and Tanya are becoming friends. I hope I see a lot more of you."

I smiled and stared in his eyes, not his crotch. His eyes, but I wanted to sneak another peek.

"Okay, please get out of here now," he ordered. I turned and pulled the door closed behind me and almost bumped into Tanya, appearing out of the shadows.

"There you are. Where is Byron?" she asked. I pointed to the stairs and continued towards them, saying nothing. I felt like I had a moment with her boyfriend and she would not be thrilled about that. I began my climb as she pushed into the bathroom to discover clean-assed Justin. He would explain the situation and she would be fine, I hoped.

The top floor was under my feet and my bladder was ready to burst like a water balloon left attached to an outside spigot too long. Byron abandoned the bathroom and probably found another girl to smooch since I'd been gone forever, but I finally had dibs on a toilet and relief was achieved.

"Damie? Hello, Damie?"

Byron was calling me incorrectly and I wasn't surprised since the basement was super loud when I shared my name. I followed his beckoning voice to a dimly lit bedroom and the cute bartender was lying on a king-sized bed with his head propped up by his hands. With his biceps popping out of his sleeves he was very sexy, and I've never thought that about anyone, including Tom Cruise.

"You kind of scared me. I thought I was in a Friday the 13th movie or something, you know, heading into a room with a hockey-masked killer," I said and laughed, nervously.

"Yeah, I don't think Jason Voorhees talks, so he wouldn't be calling you," Byron said and patted the bed, an invitation to join. He reached for my hand when I was close and pulled me onto the bed and kissed my ear. "Wanna get naked?"

The defining moment in my sexual awakening had arrived. Anticipation for a moment I thought might never happen made me shiver in the same way that lying in an igloo without a winter coat would. I wasn't sure I was ready for the winter coat.

I meant I was ready.

I thought I was maybe ready.

Byron sensed my uncertainty and kissed me, hoping the lip lock would relax me. It worked and I calmed, the winter coat fitting nicely. For five minutes we did nothing but kiss and that gave me the sense he wouldn't pressure me into more.

And then he cupped my semi-fake boobs. I jerked away in surprise.

"I'm sorry, I didn't mean to scare you," Byron said. "Don't be weird, but I know you stuffed your bra. It's okay," he said as he pulled a tissue sticking out of my left bra and blew his nose. We both laughed.

"I really needed that, thank you so much. Your chest is like a portable box of Kleenex. It'd be cool to hang around with you when I had a cold, and a runny nose."

I punched him and laughed again.

"I know one was droopy, I was so embarrassed when I looked in the mirror," I said.

"Well, yes. Also, the toilet overflowed after you left and pieces of foam came out," Byron said, sparking another uncontrollable round of laughter as we rolled around on top of each other, playfully wrestling until exhausted.

"Don't they make padded bras? I've seen my mother wearing them. Wouldn't that be easier to wear?" I was getting boob enhancement advice from a strange boy who stared at his half-naked mom. I sat up but he gently pushed me back and slowly kissed me.

I was comfortable again and didn't jump the second time he felt me up. That led to more rolling on the bed and each time I did a complete roll I lost an article of clothing. If I were Wonder Woman spinning, I'd be completely naked and not wearing the shiny blue and red underwear that superhero wore. Also, they wouldn't show on Primetime television the things Byron did to me with his tongue and his hands.

He whispered in my ear, *can I put it in,* and I knew what the "*it*" was as it rubbed against my leg like one of those big pretzels the barber guy gave Theo after a shitty buzz cut. I thought about being pregnant in high school, like three other girls in my grade and asked if he had a rubber. He did not but assured me he would pull out before that messy thing happened. He also convinced me I wouldn't get pregnant since I was a virgin.

"How did you know I was a virgin?" I asked him since he didn't go to my school and shouldn't know my reputation.

"It's pretty obvious. I can feel your body shivering a little."

"Maybe I'm just cold?"

"No. It's more than that. Your legs are like glued together—they don't want to spread even an inch. Look, it's okay. I know how to do this. I won't hurt you," he said and nibbled on my neck which felt so good. He really did know what he was doing and it was the next best thing besides being with a boy I loved. He was a professor of lust and I needed to pass his course with an A, for Arousing and not an F for Fizzle.

I relaxed my thighs and allowed my innocence to be taken, as my mother referred to losing virginity. Just because I engaged in sex didn't mean all innocence was lost. Other aspects of my life were still innocent, excluding the stolen knapsack and getting head-butted by a severed hand, of course. I was sure to encounter more moments in my young life that would crack my childhood like an egg and push me to maturation. Everything happened so quickly at the party and I kept thinking about Justin sitting on the toilet as I was having sex for the first time with a total stranger. I worried Devisha would be mad that I didn't get her approval.

I screamed and opened my eyes, eliminating all the people and distracting thoughts in my head. Something felt weird down yonder.

"I'm sorry, are you okay?" Byron asked as he stopped for a moment. I chuckled and told him it felt wonderful. His hips resumed, barely missing a thrust while I ground my teeth and wished my mouth guard was near—afraid the jaw pressure would shatter an incisor or molar. He tried to sneak his tongue back in my mouth but entry could turn him to a mute. As painful and uncomfortable as the moment was, I'd be relieved the label and expectation would disappear come morning. Conversations about sex between my classmates would not be awkward to hear and take part in now because I understood. I could hold my own in sex education. Sex equated popularity, or at least gave kids an edge, and now that I conquered it, I was free to concentrate on academics. I laughed at that thought.

"Did I suck that bad?" Byron asked as he dressed, my laugh sparking insecurity. I assured him he didn't suck and as I sat up and looked for my underwear, I noted the décor of the bedroom. The oak headboard was as tall as the ceiling and the family pics on the nightstand and the countless angel figurines judged me from every corner of the burgundy colored room. I lost my virginity on the bed of Justin's parents, the information used against me years later when I confessed to Justin after we married. Turned out he never washed the sheets before they returned from the Bahamas.

"I'm moving to Pennsylvania next week. My dad got a job there," Byron said as he slid back into his shirt. I wasn't sure to be happy our love affair was dead or act disappointed that he wouldn't become obsessed with me and want to make sweet love to me every day.

"Bummer. Maybe we can hang out before you leave? Will you be back to visit?" I asked, wanting to seem interested in seeing him again but also not caring to ever see him again. Nailing down an emotion was hard as my innards were burning.

"I doubt I'll be back. And I won't have time to hang. But this was fun. I'll never forget this night. It was magical. Goodbye, Damie." He kissed me on the cheek and left the room and the door wide open for everyone to see my half naked body. I was no longer bothered by my lack of interest as I pushed the door into Devisha's face. It slowly creaked open and my bestie stepped in the room. She looked me up and down as I covered my titter tots with my hands, she seemed as shocked with my sluttiness as I was shocked for her appearing out of nowhere.

"Oh my god. You did it with that bartender, didn't you?"

I started to cry, overcome with the implications of what happened, the shame and guilt, but also the happiness and relief. She hugged me for a minute and joined in the cry, a little of our fight from earlier creeping in and I apologized. Devisha helped dress me as I told her everything and she promised me the pain was perfectly normal the first time and I would be ready for more of the nasty soon. I disagreed and she congratulated me for beating Fruit of the Loom boy to the bedroom. My party certainly ended differently than Martin's party.

After we gathered all the tissues spread out on the bed, we decided to escape any awkward follow-ups with Byron or anyone he might have bragged to and sneaked out of the party. Devisha worked the in-crowd and planted seeds of friendships she hoped grew into beautiful orchids of popularity next school year. The only thing that grew for me in the days following the party was a bad case of gonorrhea and I was grateful to never see Byron again.

Word that I was a guaranteed lay made the rounds in the fall and the popularity I desired came mostly from the boys thinking they could score with me. Tanya was nice to my face and invited me to sit with the popular group at lunch and football games but I later discovered she was spreading lies about me because of my bathroom encounter with her boyfriend. Jealousy destroyed the chance of a genuine friendship with Tanya, and jealousy ended her relationship with Justin which allowed him to pursue the girl of his dreams. *That would be me*. I never retaliated against Tanya or exposed her shopping trips to Newman's Garbage, as I caught her buying garbage several more times over the years.

Back in present time I swallowed my last bite of tuna sandwich and shuddered at the horror of my youth—of how perception clouded any form of correct decision-making. What was the harm if I saved myself for marriage? That would've been an honorable thing. I wished my mom allowed nurturing, thoughtful conversations regarding sex but that wasn't a topic she wanted to discuss unless it was to nag me it was bad. Of course, if she came in my room and started discussing lubrication and proper lovemaking form, I would've jumped out the window.

Justin kept in touch with Byron after his move to Pennsylvania but they disconnected when Byron fell into a life of crime. He ran over a guy in a supermarket parking lot years later in Ohio and ended up in prison for drug trafficking. A few years after that he was one of nine people who were kidnapped and dumped in a landfill in Illinois. That ordeal finally did him in, his body found just outside the landfill as he was close to escaping death but unable to avoid the journey to the dark side. I journeyed to a different dark side after my experience with him. My dark side was psychological, filled with regret and self-loathing and painful urination. Hearing of his death brought a tinge of sadness for him; his loss of innocence resulted from being a boy in the world with zero guidance.

Ten minutes later I pulled in the driveway to find my parent's garage door open, exposing my father's horrible hoarding for the world to see. From a riding horse on springs to rusty, old appliances, to unlabeled water-stained boxes containing unknown crap. These were some of many piles that filled the space around the old Ford Taurus parked in the middle of the two-car garage. Queasiness hit me when I realized it would take months to sort through the stacks. I wanted to pitch it all in the dumpster but Theo forbade it. He was due to arrive and help at some point, but never gave me a firm date.

"What the hell is this, mom?" Abigail asked as she entered the garage from the side door leading to the kitchen. She was holding my Stoli vodka bottle. I hadn't realized I drank nearly the entire bottle last night. I also forgot to hide the evidence behind the old frozen meats in the freezer.

"That was already here," I lied.

"Bullshit. There was no alcohol in this house. I made sure of that before you got here." She had me. I had nothing to fire back. No other fork in the road to travel to convince her I had not fallen off the wagon. The cold truth was going to hit me across the face again.

I was an alcoholic.

CHAPTER NINE: SWIMMING WITH THE FISH

My daughter staged an intervention three months back and I was clean until a few weeks ago. Justin left when he discovered I was drinking again. He got the hell out quicker than a doe fleeing the forest after a gunshot. It was my fifth attempt at sobriety in my life—*in our lives*, as each time I fell off the wagon he plunged with me. I spiraled again when my dad's health took a turn for the worst. Justin warned me at the last intervention he couldn't handle another relapse, so it wasn't a surprise he left. The irony of my addiction—it began in the basement of his house thirty-five years ago. It wasn't alcoholism until much later in my life, but the seeds were planted at that party. Justin argued the seeds planted were literally marijuana, and that the green plant was my gateway drug. I never went back to marijuana as a substitute for alcohol during my sobriety attempts.

I was secretly pleased when Justin packed his two suitcases and fled. The relapse was easier to hide from everyone else with him gone. But I assured him I would overcome my disease again and begged him not to tell anyone, and he kept mum, presumably because he felt guilty for leaving me in my millionth time of need.

Abigail suspected I slipped when she grilled me about her father yesterday. She couldn't wait to get back to the house today to find the evidence as she enjoyed playing the private detective; of gathering clues and hunches so she could prove I was guilty of being a weak human. She uncovered my incapability of controlling my urges, and because she kept her life together so well it was easy to judge me for being a screw-up.

"How long?" Abigail asked, and the two-words formed such a simple question. How long was the drive to Nashville? How long until Christmas? How long until the new season of The Handmaid's Tale? These were the questions that followed "How long" in a healthy family. In my family it always meant *how long* was I drinking again.

"Three weeks, dear. But I'm okay. I'm not going to end up in the bushes out back, I promise. I just needed a little something to get me through all of this stress," I said, pointing to the surrounding filth in the garage.

"You're an alcoholic mom, this is not okay. Drinking as a coping mechanism is one way you will never recover. We've had this discussion. Come on inside and I'll find an AA group around here."

"No, not inside. Call out here, please. I don't want to be humiliated in front of Mateo."

"He understands. His brother is an addict."

An addict. I hated that word. Sounded like something vile. Something you'd brush against in a dark sewer in a Stephen King novel.

"Every family has one, right?" I asked, trying to normalize it through sarcasm. My pride took a brutal punch every time my alcohol drought ended.

"There's no such thing as a perfect family. You've met Mateo's mom. She has a severe paranoia problem. Every weird sound she hears outside means someone is coming to kill her. That is no lie. She genuinely thinks that. She's in therapy to overcome that. Just like you're going to AA to overcome your problem."

My problem. Abigail wasn't convinced I had a disease.

"Has she been told to quit the serial killer obsessions? How many times did she watch that Ted Bundy movie on Netflix? Yeah, every family has their lunatic." I walked past her and she followed me inside. Sitting on the kitchen counter was one of those one-cup coffee makers, the high-end brand. Also occupying the counter were several variety cases of coffee pods and an assortment of energy drinks, diet sodas, and a case of bottled water. It did help to have a variety of beverage options to keep the brain from the booze; I just couldn't think of them as mixers for cocktails.

The liquid buffet was beautiful and love was the force behind the display.

I hugged Abigail and bit my lower lip to keep from crying. I had to stop disregarding Justin's feelings and hurting my family, although Theo wasn't affected as he never attended the interventions or sibling support groups.

After Abigail's embrace, I wanted a hug from Mateo, who had been spreading out the drinks on the counter. I used every opportunity for his beefy chest to overtake mine and recognized it was a cheap thrill, but I couldn't recall the last time Justin squeezed me and transferred that kind of comfort.

"And ten minutes later my fifty year old mother was mysteriously pregnant," Abigail joked, prompting Mateo to release me. I chuckled and asked the location of the little one with the bruised noggin and Abigail pointed to my old room. She then held her phone in front of my face, showing the location of a local AA meeting. One was conveniently scheduled for that afternoon. I nodded and smiled, but I hated the thoughts of the tedious ritual.

To shift the mood of the room a bit, I shared the conversation I had with Chuck the night before and showed them the love letter hidden behind the fish.

"This doesn't mean grandpa was gay or anything, mom. This was a sign of respect. He respected his friend's feelings and kept it between the two of them so it wasn't exposed and minimized to the world," Abigail said, her interpretation differing from mine. It certainly would be a noble thing to keep to oneself, but who's to say mother didn't know. Mateo told us his good friend was bisexual, which seemed to surprise Abigail. This led to an argument about whether he told her this information years ago, and the scene could have played out similarly had my dad shared Chuck's story with my mom.

As the hushed disagreement continued, I snuck in my old room and grabbed the knapsack and admired my napping granddaughter, then snatched the trout to take to the UPS hub up the street. Abigail sternly reminded me to go to the AA meeting and I nodded as I blew a kiss and slid out the front door.

After I set the fish free in a sea of UPS boxes, I had an hour to kill and debated swinging by a bar and grabbing one last double rum and coke before the AA meeting like I'd done before. One last swig for the rest of my life. Seemed cruel to not be allowed to do something you loved ever again in your life. Such was the bitch called sobriety.

I passed a sign for Ant Falls—a local park with gorgeous waterfalls, where I could murder my hour easily. Dev and I spent a bunch of time there and I remembered visiting the park the weekend after Justin's sex party. We had the neon knapsack with us that day as well.

I parked and located the same big rock we called home. It was now surrounded by brush but was still accessible by a little footpath. I sat and looked across the creek at a flock of geese splashing in the water. A huge cluster of clouds hid the sun, which was fine with me as the temperature was flirting with eighty degrees and I didn't want to fry like bacon on a griddle. The familiarity of the location soothed me and the only thing missing was my former best friend. We grew apart throughout high school and after graduation I moved to college and married Justin. We reconnected on Facebook five years ago, but besides having 'friends' status on social media Devisha and I didn't communicate. I wasn't even sure she still lived in Sundown; her social media information was incomplete.

"And then pop went your cherry!"

"Pop? More like an explosion. I'm still in pain, you know," I said as I carefully lowered my butt onto the big rock that touched the rushing water coming off Ant Falls. "It feels kind of itchy down there, too." I hadn't yet discovered the loss of my virginity yielded an unpleasant infection. Devisha dragged me to the free clinic on Wednesday of the next week. Fortunately, the physician on site was filling in from out of town, so word in our small town never spread, unlike the gonorrhea Byron gave me.

"Was this in here or did you put it in here?" Devisha was holding a hunting knife by the handle but the blade hid in the leather sheath. We didn't see the dried blood on it until later. I shook my head, indicated it was in the bag. "Why would boy pack a knife?" I shrugged and looked through the other objects that were spread across the rock. A couple t-shirts; one plain, one with the rock band The Clash. Besides the Fruit of the Loom undies, a pair of Levi jeans and a couple pairs of gym shorts made up the only articles of clothing in the bag. Martin was quite the light packer. A deck of cards, a pack of Hubba Bubba gum, a comb, sunglasses, a map of Tennessee and a pencil rounded out the contents of the neon knapsack. Typical travel items, I supposed, except for the knife. Maybe it was normal for a young guy traveling alone to pack a weapon for protection.

"Okay, I'm going to randomly pick a page to read from," Devisha said as she fanned the journal pages for a moment and then stopped on a page about three-quarters of the way through. About a year after the Escape Club Tragedy and the Dance of the Dead.

"Take Me Home. Maybe Marty finally gets himself a family!"

Take Me Home
November 21, 1984

Two weeks gone and still no Adam. I'm not sure why I thought he would be back.

A welcoming family chose him two weeks ago after they had interviewed five of us boys. I was nothing but honest in my interview because they seemed like a nice couple. (Other couples seemed weird sometimes, so I would lie about how bad I was or about how much trouble I got into or flunking school, or anything.) They were older but so am I compared to the kids under thirteen. Anyone who chooses me only gets five years before I am outta there! With Adam (the younger choice) they would have more time with him. Some of the questions they ask:

#1 What was your home life like?
Well, it was great. Except for my parents getting killed in a skiing accident when I was eight. They decided they didn't need instructions and tried to go down a steep hill that was not part of the ski path and they

ended up skiing off a cliff and into a frozen ravine. They were missing for a month before their bodies were found, after everything had thawed out. "Oh, that is terrible, we are quite sorry, Martin." Not as sorry as I was. Especially when I had to live with my Uncle Jackass II. (They would look at me with shock, I always enjoyed the different reactions. Some possible parents were shocked, some seemed disgusted, and some laughed. The ones that laughed I thought would be cool parents to have so they would ask more stories of **UJ-2**) He was so dumb he once tried cooking a chicken in the microwave. And I don't mean a frozen chicken, I mean he took one of the neighbor's chickens, since we lived next to a farm, in a crappy cabin, and he sawed the head off with a steak knife, cut the legs off and put it in the microwave and cooked it for about five minutes. It exploded in there. (I would laugh. They might laugh. It was kind of a gross out story.)

#2 Let's go back to your parents. When they were alive what types of things did you do as a family? Which activities did you enjoy doing?

Ski diving and crocodile wrangling.

(More shocked and surprised looks.)

I'm just kidding, I would tell them. Then I would stick with the truth. We didn't do a lot together, the three of us. I did not have any brothers or sisters and my dad traveled a bunch. My mom and me would go to the zoo once a year. That was always fun. One year we went to Hastings Beach, a couple hours in the car. The three of us went and I had a good time playing in the sand. Making a sand fortress and swimming. This was the only vacation I remembered. Outside of the flat in London, we didn't travel as a family. I think that was because my dad already flew a lot in his job he didn't feel like it when he wasn't working. My dad never talked about his work. When I asked him about it he would say it was boring money stuff.

My mum didn't work but she stayed busy. She did a lot with friends. She had tons of friends and she would always take me to their houses to visit and I would play with their kids. That was fun. That was an activity I enjoyed doing with my mum, but it really wasn't with her it was with the kids I got to play with. It was the swing sets and the horses and the pools. Besides boring school, this was the most I left the flat. So I would say visiting and playing with my mum's friends kids was the activity I liked the best.

#3 Did you miss doing more things with your mummy and daddy? Would you have liked to do more with them?

This seemed like a stupid question. Of course I would have liked to do more stuff with them. I never felt I really knew my dad. I cried more for my mum dying and even with her it felt more of a presence. A life force. I don't remember having cuddling or affection. She taught me things, almost like my school teachers. She tucked me in bed at night and told me she loved me but it would feel like a school teacher. Like I could hear my art class teacher Miss Evermore saying she loved me. I always felt cared for, I guess, and that seemed to be enough.

#4 What sorts of things would you like to do with your new parents?

This was a tough question. But also an easy question. There was so much outside of our small London flat and I feel like I never really did much of anything so I guess I would want to travel and see the world, just like my dad. I would want to travel and spend more time with my new parents. I would try every flavor of ice cream that was ever made. I would ride the biggest and tallest roller coaster. I would ride a two wheeler through the woods. I would play football and baseball. I never really had a chance to do any of these things. With my dad being gone it was hard for my mum to schedule everything herself.

#5 Would you like a brother or sister?

~~HELL~~ yeah I would like a brother or sister. I would love someone to boss around and pick on but also to play with and stuff. It would be a lot less lonely. I think a sister would be better. I could be protective of her. A big brother who would kick anyone's ass that tried to mess with her, that's what I would be...

Those were the questions most asked. I thought I answered mostly okay, for the couples I most liked, anyway. I thought I gave some damn good interviews so it confused me when I was never picked. I'm 13 now and have been at Chatterbee for 3 years. I'm not getting any younger, as Lady Asswipe would tell me before every interview. She was pushing to get me out. I was one of the oldest there and it probably looked bad on her if nobody wanted me. Like she couldn't make me wantable. A welcoming family did not find me welcoming, she would say. Smile and be happy, she would tell me, after I would hear about another little boy being sent down in the basement to the crate. How did that make me happy?

What would make me happy would be telling a couple in an interview about the crate and what Henshaw did to punish us boys and girls. Getting that out and having someone tell the police would be great, but Henshaw was there for every interview. She would not allow that to happen. Everyone was afraid of her and afraid of never getting out of Chatterbee. Doing well in the interview was important more for them than for her. My best friend, Adam, must have done very well in his interview two weeks ago. He was gone. It seemed he would not be returned on bad behavior and how could he? He was one of the best here. I was happy for him but very sad. I did not have anyone as a best friend back up. My roommate Brandon was still annoying and his gas problem was even worse than before. I really wished they would stop serving beans at every stinking meal. I never saw myself as best friends with him. It just would never happen. What really sucked horse-dick was I wouldn't even be here if it wasn't for my bloody worthless uncle. Uncle Jackass II could have saved me from this life if he had been a capable guardian but **NOOOO** he got himself thrown in jail for burning down a house. He was paid by a jilted husband to burn down the house of their ex-wife while she was asleep but she woke and tackled him after he lit a corner of the inside of the house near the fireplace. She dragged him out and pummeled him while the house burnt down. So now, here I sit in my bed, 3am, while Brandon farts in his sleep, the sound and the stench keeping me from even dreaming about a life I could have someday.

Someday.

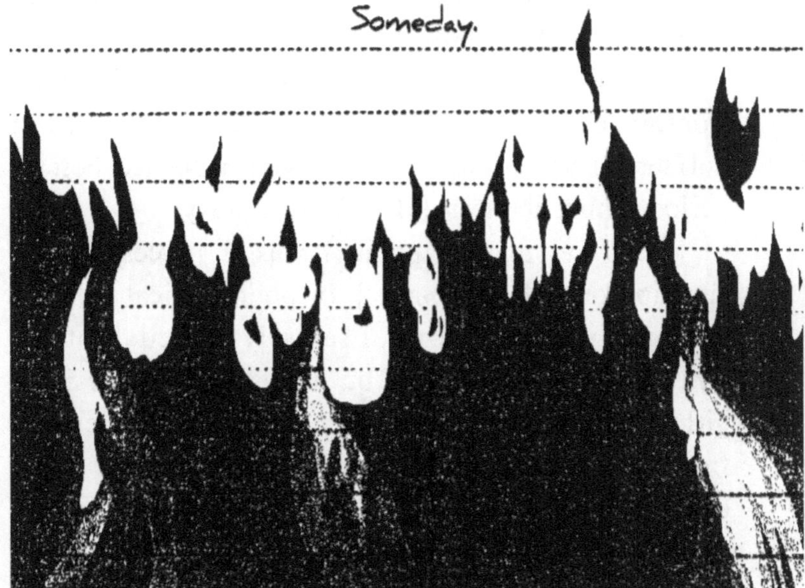

"If that isn't the saddest shit I've ever read," Devisha said as she handed me the journal. We sprawled out on the rock, under the glowing sun that seemed to be right on top of us. The sound of the falls in the distance and an occasional splash of water against the rock made for a relaxing visit to Ant Falls that afternoon. "Why do you think you found this bag, Mamie?"

"I don't know. It stood out. The neon green was bright, I saw it from far away."

"No. I meant what does it mean for you, is it a sign of some sort? You gettin anything from these stories of this boy? His life?" She would start talking religious stuff, I felt it coming. She and her family were big into church and praising Jesus and stuff.

"I guess I haven't really thought about it that way."

"Well, start thinking, girl. This has got to mean something to you. This has to be a sign or a lesson of some kind. I mean, how many people in the world ever, I mean EVER have the chance to find a bag left behind from someone who may be dead from a plane crash? I'm not sure if something like that even happened before, period. Think about that. It's fucking crazy."

That was a great point. I wasn't processing the situation on a deep, spiritual, or philosophical level. It was merely surface for me. I selfishly wanted this to be a mystery or an adventure but I was a fifteen-year-old girl who wanted to be popular in school and independent from my family. I also wanted a boyfriend and a tattoo of a sunflower on my calf. I was as shallow as dog piss on a sidewalk during a drought.

"Dig deeper."

She was reading my mind. Dev was intuitive.

"I get it. I'm digging deeper on some spiritual level."

"You should come with me to church tomorrow," Devisha suggested as she stood up on the rock and began to mimic her priest or preacher or whatever you called them. "And the Lord Jesus said unto you, look not badly onto those who are struggling but open your arms to them. Welcome them into your home and feed them oatmeal and vanilla wafers. Give to them Sunny Delight orange juice and a wash rag to scrub their stinking behinds. Let them covet your wife or husband and love them all the more. For this I praise the Lord," and then she screamed, "Halleluiah!"

"You are a twisted heathen. But I get your point. I'll dig deeper."

"Let's dive deeper into this nasty green water, girl thang! It's time to swim with the fishes, bitches. Cleanse your soul, in God's name!" She took off her t-shirt and dove into the creek with only a bra and a tight pair of soccer shorts.

A splash of creek water hit my face and tore me from the past and my vision of my bestie swimming with the fish and the geese droppings. I never did jump in after Devisha because for someone who longed for adventure, I was not always quick to take the adventure. Maybe the water cleansing the soul was no joke and my soul could've benefited from the swim. Maybe my life would've been more peaceful.

Clouds reflected in the water and encouraged me to reflect in a spiritual, deeper level on the thirty-five years since my last visit to the falls. How did I get to the point of chemical dependency, and could I ever escape it? Would I uncover a sincerity in the life of Martin that would push me to dig deeper?

At least one of those questions would be answered in the next couple hours.

CHAPTER TEN: COFFEE AND DONUTS

My career in hospitality rarely saw meetings held in a hotel. AA meetings were typically held in the basements of churches or old banquet rooms at a rec center or grade-school cafeterias. These locations were sometimes just as downtrodden as the people sitting in circles sharing misery stories. I've visited many locations with countless faces of those fighting alcoholism and I desperately believed alcoholism was a disease, as did most attendees, because this identification meant it was curable. Unfortunately, many outsiders viewed unhealthy drinking as a choice—likely because they didn't over indulge or they had superiority complexes. Just because Joe Schmo can limit his number of rum and cokes to two or three and only drinks on weekends doesn't mean we can follow suit. Addiction can be a genetic thing, although in my situation I didn't see the signs. My parents weren't big drinkers; I don't recall ever seeing them out-of-control drunk and they never shared stories of anyone else in the family having that problem. I suspected I had a predisposition to addictive behaviors, or an addictive personality. Smoking pot daily as a teenager proved that theory.

As I walked down the stairs to the basement of the Holy Trinity Methodist Church in the slums of Sundown, I smelled mold or mildew or something indicating the building was as old as dirt. I once caught the same smell in my bedroom and saturated the room with air fresheners of all shapes and sizes. It was like walking in a field of wild flowers if the field had electrical outlets on the ground and Glade plug-ins were attached throughout. The habit of camouflaging gross odors came in handy when I started lighting up.

Hitting the ground level of the church, the moldy aroma became pleasant smells of coffee and pastries, another staple in the world of the anonymous alcoholic. I took a deep breath before opening the double doors, my anxiety high for several reasons. I hated the tedious retelling of my stories as they bored the hell out of me, but this meeting had me more anxious about running into someone I knew. This was a fear that haunted me every time I visited my parents, for they were the only reason I returned to Sundown. I didn't keep in touch with anyone from school when Justin and I moved to Chicago, and I never attended a reunion. Being in town forced me to relive the insecurities of my childhood, even though I had overcome most of them as an adult. These worries prevented me from coming back and spending time with my parents as they aged and that was unfortunate.

I pulled the large metal handle on the door but it didn't open. I tried again with more force, and it not only opened it detached from its hinges. I screamed and ran to avoid losing a limb as the wrought iron door fell with a thud, sending dust and dirt scattering like the munchkins from the wicked witch. Half of the double-door entry was now missing.

"Didn't you read the sign, lady?" A girl asked, appearing from the other side of the fallen door. She was young, I guessed twenty, and she wore a hooded sweatshirt with a Sundown High School Hog embroidery, the hog being the school mascot, as if the town needed to display it's backwoods status. I looked down at the door and read the sign, "Please do not enter here. Please use the other set of doors," with an arrow pointing right. Apparently, there was another set of doors down the hall that would've allowed me to enter the confessional without destroying the property of the church.

"Oops," I chuckled nervously, as the pencil-thin girl rolled her heavily mascaraed eyes and walked away, offering zero assistance. As I bent to raise the door another pair of much larger hands pitched in to help. These hands were illustrated; one with a machine gun and one with a grenade; anger issues displayed proudly.

"Lean it," the bald, behemoth of a man said, and I obeyed. After we placed the door safely against the wall the man introduced himself as Alex and extended his grenade, or his right hand. I shook and studied his face for a moment. He didn't look like an Alex, more like a Rambo, or a Bruce or a Rock. I smiled and thanked him, relieved he wasn't a former classmate, but didn't share my name, unsure if I would share my real name at this meeting. He smiled back, exposing a silver grill across the front of his upper teeth. He'd easily pass for a villain in a superhero movie, his look completed by jeans and black leather vest. I didn't think Sundown bred humans like him. He motioned for me to follow him into the dimly lit cafeteria and the circle of chairs where two seats were already occupied. The hooded girl slouched in one chair while an older woman, dressed very nicely with styled, gray hair, sat straight up in another.

I followed Alex Rambo to the refreshments table and noticed another tattoo on his forearm—it was a hunting knife similar to the one in Martin's knapsack. He was too mellow to be displaying such aggression on his skin. I wanted to ask if he'd slaughtered anyone but that wasn't the right time or place, so I remained tight-lipped. He nudged me and pointed to a pink frosted donut with multi-colored sprinkles. I smiled and looked up at him as he nodded slowly as if to say, "That donut is the shit.

Choose that donut." Wanting to please him I reached for the donut but he quickly snatched it and shoved the entire thing in his mouth. He laughed as he swallowed—which seemed an impossible feat, and five seconds later he sat in the circle of chairs. I stood in a daze, processing this odd encounter. If he wanted me to try the donut, why did he take it? There was only one of its kind on the table, so this action seemed cruel. The Avengers would punish him in their next film.

Skipping other donut choices, I grabbed a coffee and made my way to a cold, metal chair. I appreciated meeting spaces with poor lighting; it was easier to admit you're damaged goods without a spotlight shining down on your head.

As was common with smaller head counts, each of us sat as far as possible from each other. I snuck glances at faces, trying to guess which clichés matched each of them from similar stories I've heard. The Sundown Hog looked around the room like she was watching a species of Finch flying over. Having studied Finches during my bird-watching phase ten years ago, I'd like to guess it was a Zebra Finch—they were the coolest. She was high or scarred from alcohol abuse, which was heartbreaking to see, being so young. The nicely dressed elderly woman didn't match an AA cliché, she matched a group leader cliche. Alex was mid-thirties and decent looking in a scary way. He could snap my one hundred-thirty-pound body like a twig, and that violent image played as he caught me staring and smiled, his frosted pink upper lip causing me to smile back as I sipped my disgusting coffee. I gazed back at the older woman, expecting her to begin the group, as it was time. She started texting, quickly tapping her phone with her pointer fingers. I was impressed with her speed. I sensed her a sweet lady and she made me miss my mom.

"Fuckin idiot!" she said as she shook her head and rolled her eyes.

I giggled as she blew my character assessment of her out of the water. Alex and the girl with the hoody didn't flinch.

"I told her to unplug the air fryer and she didn't. The damn thing caught on fire and she had to figure out how to use the fire extinguisher. Only she didn't figure out how to use the fire extinguisher. I just gave her a lesson on how to use that son-of-a-bitchin thing three days ago."

"So, what then, your place burnt down?" the girl asked.

"Fuck if it did. No! She threw water on it. And then she slipped in the water and smashed her knee on the god-damn floor!"

I was still finding humor to the story but I was missing some information. "Who are you talking about?" I asked.

"My dumbass crippled sister. She's not even supposed to leave the recliner when I'm not home. I get out of that stinking apartment twice a god-damn week and she can't stay still."

"She outta be euthanized," hoody girl said and I was shocked by these people, once again. I learned conclusions shouldn't be made by appearances. "I'm fuckin with you Granny Smith!" she said as Alex snorted twice and then revisited the snack table. He came back with a chocolate-covered donut. That poor pastry survived all of three seconds in his machine-gun hand. Queen could've based one of their biggest hits on those poor donuts. *Another One Bites the Dust*. It was now ten minutes past our start time. Granny Smith evidently was not the leader.

"Good afternoon."

A woman's voice was heard before she surfaced from the darkness on the other side of the basement cafeteria. When she hit the circle of light my heart tried to belly-flop out of my chest and my fear of running into someone I knew from high school became justified.

It was Devisha.

I was stunned as I recalled a standard comment on Facebook profile pictures: *You look exactly the same as you did in high school*. Many experiences with my former best friend swam in my mind like a bucket of minnows. I felt like I was sitting in a desert as my face flushed and I started to sweat. Devisha looked at the group, stopping her gaze at me and staring for a questionable amount of time but I wasn't sure she recognized me. I was a much lighter adult, both in stature and hair but my boobs were bigger without stuffing from an outdoor cushion. Besides a few added wrinkles, my face looked the same. Still, even if she identified me, this was supposed to be an anonymous setting and she wouldn't call me out.

Devisha picked up a note card and started reading the preamble, "Alcoholics Anonymous is a fellowship of men and women who share their experience, strength and hope with each other that they may solve their common problem and help others to recover from alcoholism." She continued about no dues and contributions as I stared at her hard, waiting for her to look at me again and give me some sort of acknowledgement of recognition.

"Our primary purpose is to stay sober and help other alcoholics to achieve sobriety," Devisha concluded. The preamble was seared into my brain and I knew what the next order of preaching would be if we were attending a typical twelve-step AA meeting. She asked us to stand and join hands and we all joined in with "God grant me the Serenity to accept the things I cannot change, Courage to change the things I can, and Wisdom to know the difference."

The group was practicing a faith-based AA which wasn't my favorite since I never became a spiritual, God-fearing woman. It was amusing my best friend from high school who pushed church and spirituality on me back in our heyday would get another shot at it in adulthood. I wasn't sure if this time around my life was messier, but a case could be made that I should've listened to Dev and turned to God instead of booze. Now I needed to make up for lost time, I needed faith to save my life. Or so she would suggest.

"Let's start by welcoming our newcomer and allow her the opportunity to introduce herself to the group."

Devisha looked at me and smiled and I still wasn't convinced she knew who the hell I was. Declining the intro and not sharing was allowed, but that was never helpful for me. Listening to stories of alcohol abuse and arrests and beating kids and cheating on spouses did not inspire me to do better since I never related with those stories or did those terrible things. Sharing my stories proved (at least to myself) I wasn't that bad and achieving sobriety would not be difficult. I realized that sounded like I was better than everyone else which was the reason I never shared those thoughts out loud. I did know others worse off than me had achieved sobriety more solidly, so I wasn't better than anyone. But I needed to be better than my current self.

"Hello, I'm, ummm, I'm Scarlett,"

I didn't say I was an alcoholic because I didn't have to say that. Nobody attending the meeting was forced to label themselves as anything and just because I fell off the wagon didn't mean I broke a hip and would take forever to recover; I merely sprained an ankle.

"Hello Scarlett," everyone said together, with little enthusiasm. They seemed annoyed I was there, but I wouldn't take it personally. Still, I was amazed there were only three addicts in Sundown. Maybe there was a high school sporting event happening.

"What brings you to our meeting today, Scarlett?" Devisha asked, making things even weirder—my former best friend was addressing me by the name of the heroine from Gone with the Wind, a movie we watched countless times together on VHS tape. This connection wasn't aglow in her eyes, though.

"I fell on hard times and I lost control of my alcohol consumption."

"Well, we're here to listen and encourage you to maintain your sobriety. We also hope you are not too hard on yourself, that you are forgiving yourself for giving in to alcohol," Devisha said.

"Also, my daughter made me come. I'm doing this to satisfy her just as much as me," I said, not really planning to admit that.

"Satisfying family members is motivation to stop using, and I'm happy to hear you are also wanting to help yourself. Helping yourself will help your daughter and will give you the freedom from feeling guilty for sneaking behind her back."

"You seem to have all the answers," I said with immediate regret, not understanding why I was picking a fight with her. Maybe because I was hurt that she didn't recognize someone who meant the world to her half a lifetime ago.

"I do not have all the answers. That is why I am here as well. I am here to lead the group and to gather the strength that you all bring here to provide me the warmth and protection I need to keep me from a relapse."

All eyes were on me except for hooded girl, who was rolling her eyes again. I never considered Devisha was present as a recovering alcoholic. I never thought she'd go down the same rabbit hole. I was a horrible person.

"Oh. I'm sorry," I said, hoping for a crumb of forgiveness.

"Would you like to share anything else right now?" Devisha asked and I shook my head and looked at the black scuff marks on the vinyl floor. I felt Alex's eyes on me and wondered if he wanted another donut.

"Let's move on to our topic for today's meeting. Amends. Making Hard Amends. Would anyone like to share a story about how they have made amends or how they would like to make amends to someone they love?"

"I would like to share a story," I quickly said, desperately feeling the need to express myself before I lost the nerve. Similar to volunteering to be first to stand to do speech assignments in school. The anticipation of being the fifth or twentieth student to stand in front of class was horrifying.

"Okay, why don't you share a story, Mamie," Devisha said and then gasped and turned away from me. She exposed me and I didn't care. I was happy she knew me.

"Mamie? I thought her name was Scarlett," the hooded girl said, still following the Zebra Finch to the ceiling of the cafeteria.

"Um, I'm sorry, yes, it is Scarlett, my mistake," Devisha said as she looked at me and smiled nervously.

"I would like to make amends to you, Devisha. We were best friends throughout high school, but we drifted apart senior year," I explained to the three strangers.

"It wasn't a drift so much as you tossed me out, like a used tampon," my former bestie said.

"Oh dear," the old woman said as she crossed her legs. The comparison was vulgar, but totally something Devisha would've said back in the day, which comforted me. It seemed she hadn't changed too much.

"I am sorry to you all," Devisha continued, "this is entirely inappropriate. We will talk after the meeting, um, Scarlett."

"Wait a cotton-picking minute. Aren't these meetings about sharing with each other?" Alex asked. He was able to do more than grunt and inhale pastries! "Isn't that what these meetings are all about, to listen to all kinds of stories and to support one another?" The man made his point in the deepest monotone voice I had probably ever heard.

I looked at Devisha and raised my left eyebrow like our high school English teacher, Mrs. Weiner. She smiled and we both said, "Weiner."

"Oh dear," the older woman said again.

"Okay. Should we start your introduction over again?" Devisha asked and I nodded and shrugged. She motioned to me as the newcomer, and I reintroduced myself as myself.

"Although I never expected to run into you ever again in my life, let alone at an AA meeting in Sundown, Tennessee, I am thankful that I have and that I can make amends for the way our friendship ended over thirty years ago. Look, I know I didn't have an alcohol addiction back then, but I did smoke a lot of pot, so my amends can be attributed to that dependency. Anyway, when Justin and I started dating our senior year I was suddenly part of the popular group for the right reasons. For the good reasons, not because I was considered a slut. And I guess I just felt I needed to direct all of my energy on that relationship and my new status. I mean, suddenly people looked up to me. Girls would always come to me and ask about my clothing or my hair or my make-up. I honestly felt like a celebrity. I'm not saying it was right, but we were kids. Immature little assholes." I looked down to the ground, feeling the pain of losing my best friend, of replacing her with a boy who would end up being my husband. Replacing her with a status. I took a deep breath and looked back up at Devisha. "I'm so sorry, Dev." She looked away to compose herself and reengaged with a look of anger and hurt.

"I have a few things to say to you, Mamie. You talk about girls looking up to you for your fashion sense and what not, but who helped you find that fashion? I was still going with you to the thrift store and keeping it quiet even after you told your new best friend, Tanya, that I shopped there. Yeah, I knew you did that. You stabbed me in the back with the biggest butcher knife in the kitchen drawer, girl! And Tanya was the one that spread the slut rumor about you and then you're besties with her? That was whack! Need I remind you I was also on the verge of popularity, but when you rose above and started dragging my name through the mud my status went to shit. I gave you the runway, hoping we'd be on that plane together, but you took off and never returned," she paused and took a deep breath, "I don't want to hold you responsible because, obviously being in AA myself,

I have had my own issues, but losing you was the beginning of my downward spiral. So, yes, I accept your apology and appreciate you making amends, but I honestly, um. Thank you for the apology."

I never understood the extent of what I had done. I remembered telling Tanya stuff, but I never did it to purposely hurt Devisha. I took part in the gossip that the other girls created but felt pressured to do so. I realized the ridiculousness in the excuse but when you're young everything is so dramatic. Hearing that our failed friendship played a role in breaking her and leading her to addiction made me sick to death. So many years gone but the truth brought the pain back like the return of an illness you thought was in remission.

"Hug it out, bitches," the old woman said.

"Wait a minute. Are you talking about Tanya Spencer?" Hoody asked and I nodded. "That's my mother!" she exclaimed and I was amazed at how many strange coincidences were piling on me.

"Oh. Yes. I see a resemblance. You have a pretty face, like your mom," I offered.

"She's a bitch and I hate her. Sounds like she's always been a bitch. And you all were toxic back in the day."

Devisha and I stared at each other and she said, "Yes. Yes, we were. The sins of the past. The only way to heal and move on is to accept we are different people today and as kids we were just stupid. I'm sorry if I was hard on you, Mamie."

"Get your fucking asses up and hug it out, ladies!" Granny Smith ordered and we obeyed. As I wrapped my arms around her, I remembered the last time we hugged, when she took me to the clinic and I cried after testing positive for that disgusting STD. She was there for me, through all of my crises and I shoved her aside for popularity and a stupid boy.

I held my former best pal long enough for Alex to inhale another donut, proving he was now addicted to pastries. He was never addicted to drugs or alcohol—it was a scam to get free cakes and cookies. We weren't that different as Little Debbie sat on the snack table and pointed at me while laughing like a hyena. The trip back to Sundown was more therapeutic than I expected.

Therapy was a gift we gave one another that evening and I listened to stories of the others without prejudice and minimization of their plights. Although I didn't always relate to their circumstances I supported and encouraged without cynicism. Granny Smith's real name was Bertha White, easily mistaken for Betty White and they both possessed wit and charm and an occasional inappropriate word or seven. Hoody's name was Lorrie and she was one of four children from the loins of Tanya, who never followed in her mother or father's footsteps because she was too busy popping out kids. Turned out even though her folks had amazing careers, they were deep in debt and the family couldn't afford the clothing in Nashville shops.

Prayer time ended the meeting and although I typically left before that part, I joined for the first time and something unusual happened: I felt an energy, a comforting blanket on a frigid day, and though I didn't suddenly believe in everything almighty I embraced the comfort that came from the spoken prayers.

Devisha and I had another cup of coffee after the others left and she caught me up on her life, that she was married and divorced three times and had no children, although she tried her little heart out. Failure to produce a child accelerated her existing struggles with alcohol and the ability to sustain marriages. She felt worthless as a woman and couldn't find happiness and fulfillment in a life without children. Also, current dating possibilities in Sundown were as fruitful as a grapevine in the Antarctic.

"He was out of toilet paper again; I mean what are the odds of that happening twice?"

I shared with Devisha the beginning of my life with Justin. Another party at his house during senior year and he needed butt paper, but this time I actually found a roll and didn't hand him a wet towel. He was so appreciative that he asked me out and I've been providing Charmin for him ever since.

"That man's diet was horrendous in school," I said. "One time at lunch he took money on a dare to finish the plates of everyone at the table. I think there were like six of us and we mixed everything in a pile. He ate a lot of green beans and mashed potatoes and lettuce and olives and Italian dressing and chocolate pudding. He was okay until he ate the last olive and then he exploded all over the cafeteria." I laughed. She asked how we were doing currently and I shared our struggles and how my relapses were destroying us and how I suspected he left me for another woman and was off on a beach adventure and who could blame him.

I made plans to stop at the farm she shared with her niece, and we promised to call each other when weakness visited. I never expected to make amends with Devisha, but it eliminated a heaviness hidden deep inside of me and I felt lighter. Making amends was not only the topic of that AA meeting, but it also proved to be the motivating factor of my visit and the benefits were proving emotionally and physically uplifting.

But I couldn't become complacent. I was still climbing a treacherous mountain in my bare feet.

CHAPTER ELEVEN: WELCOMING FAMILY

On the drive back to The House of Memoirs I was motivated to call Justin. Following the rush of confidence after my reconciliation with Devisha I needed to ride the wave of certainty or I might chicken out. I didn't know what to expect from him or what I expected from myself and our marriage but it was important to keep communication streaming. I doubted he would answer.

He answered after one ring.

"And hello to you, Mamie."

"Hi Justin. How's your tan coming along? Remember, SPF 30 won't keep you from burning," I said, throwing a little shade, which he may need if he was at the beach. I did realize I caused the separation and I should be more understanding, but my brain nagged me that if our marriage had been better over the years, I wouldn't be a drunkard. I certainly wasn't blaming him, though, as in AA you are taught to take responsibility for your actions.

"Yeah. I'm using the 50. No burning going on here," he said. Suddenly, I regretted opening the conversation that way as I became a victim of my own taunting. I wasn't sure if he was being flippant. "How are you doing?" he asked.

"Are you really at the beach?" I asked, failing at filtering my thoughts and my mouth.

No reply. Crickets.

Actually, the expression should be *dead crickets*. Silence.

"Never mind. I don't have the right to know. Hey, guess what? I went to AA here. You don't know what you're missing in our lovely hometown. And guess who I ran into? Devisha Watkins. It was really nice. We had a great talk and I was able to make amends with her for the way our friendship ended back in the day. For the way my idiot self treated her in high school. It feels like a heavy weight has been lifted from my shoulders, I know that sounds cliché, but it is totally true."

The crickets were not rising like the dead in Night of the Living Dead.

"You there, Justin?"

"I'm here. I'm happy you feel lighter. But you know what? I have that same weight stuck on my shoulders, and I know that I'm a muscular, powerful man, but it is wearing me down, Mamie. Do you think I'll ever know what it feels like to have it removed?"

"You left. I'm not your responsibility anymore. That weight should be gone."

"No. It doesn't work like that and you know it. Whether we're together or not I'm carrying that weight. I will always wonder if you are safe, if you are drinking and driving, if you're pulling an all-nighter with your hotel friends, if you're lying in a ditch, dead. I will always wonder if I'm gonna have to tell our kids and our grandkids that you won't be coming home, that you lost your battle with alcohol. Christ! Sometimes you're the most self-absorbed person I have ever known. Even more than my brother, and he used to jerk off in the mirror looking at himself!"

I deserved all of that, except for the visual of his three-hundred pound brother jerking off. I was a selfish person, pulling everyone I loved into my game of Truth or Dare, except I typically chose *Dare* because I was afraid of the *Truth*. I was scared to expose the ugliness that hid in the cracks and crevices of my brain, like fleas entangled in the hairs of a beloved pet.

"You seem to be off to a good start there. I suggest you get clean in Sundown, since you have an AA there. It'll take you awhile to get the house in order, it's the perfect rehab scenario, ya know? You can keep me posted with updates by sending texts. Remember, it takes twenty-one days for something to become a habit." This was a hypothesis he mentioned often.

"Actually, it's sixty-six now. It can actually take anywhere from eighteen to two-hundred-fifty-four days, averaging sixty-six," I countered, having just read an article about habits and addictions and crap about trying to be a better person.

"Okay. Let's go with the longest time frame then. That's how many months? Hold on," he fumbled with his phone, trying to find the calculator app. "Eight and a half months. Let's say the length of a pregnancy. Nine months. If you can stay sober for nine months, I'd be willing to talk about our marriage and where we go from there," he challenged. He didn't give me time to respond as he wished me luck and said goodbye. He only wanted text updates. No video conferencing or voice calls.

Our marriage might be saved if I didn't miscarry. I needed to carry the pregnancy to term and give birth to a healthy little bastard we would name *Sober*. The topic of miscarriage awakened a passage in Martin's journal.

Although a miscarriage would end my marriage, a miscarriage almost saved Martin from the orphanage in 1985.

WELCOMING FAMILY
November 15th, 1985

It finally happened. At age 14 I have finally been picked to go home with a welcoming family. I am in my new room, It's pretty big. I even have a television set in here.

The bathroom is right across the hall and I have no competition. No fake brothers or sisters. I am the only kid (kinda a kid, kinda a grown-up) in the house. My fake mom and dad are super cool. They laughed at my jokes in the interview, they said I was twisted and they liked it. Lady Henshaw seemed very surprised by their like for me. She seemed convinced they didn't want me, She even told me that after they left the room. She said something like,

You continue to disappoint me, Martin. Do you ever want to leave here? I wish you would stop talking about your Uncle Jackass II. Please stop telling those hideous stories of mutilated chickens and burning down the house. They are quite repelling. You've repelled another sweet couple today. You absolutely should be ashamed of yourself.

And then she stormed out of the room. She was on the verge of putting me in the crate, she also said before she left. And then she came back in about three minutes with the Evans couple and smiled, kinda weird, and told me they wanted to be my mommy and daddy.

I really didn't like calling anyone mommy or daddy because I wasn't four. But I jumped out of my seat and hugged them both.

My new fake dad's name is Henry and my fake mom's name is Tilda. Henry and Tilda. They are in their thirties, Henshaw had said and they had just miscarried, which I'm pretty sure means their baby died. It wasn't the first time it happened, either. They didn't have any other choice but to adopt. And here I am. I can't be miscarried unless I'm carried in their arms and they drop me. That would be sucky. Also, I weigh like 100 lbs so why the hell would they pick me up? Also, I have a big booty. Henshaw made a crack about that a couple weeks ago, too. Something like,

Quit eating everyone's food at lunch. You're turning into a real lardass. No respectful couple will want you, let alone be able to afford to feed you.

I was so happy to be away from that cunt face.

November 18th, 1985

We went to the park today. It was a little cold, but they gave me a new heavy fluffy coat and thick boots. I actually got too hot at one point. We did the swings and the merry-go-round, the same things I used to do at Chatterbee's outside play area. I still really miss Adam. I asked Tilda if we could try to find him so I could visit with him. She said she would call Chatterbee and find out.

November 20th, 1985

It is 3:30am and I can't sleep. I keep hearing someone walking around outside my door. This is the 2nd night I heard it. The steps seem heavy so I think it is Henry. Maybe he has that disease thing that keeps you awake. Or maybe he walks in his sleep. I don't really want to ask. I like my fake mom and dad, but I think we are still learning each other. We are still trying to fit in together. Sometimes at dinner none of us say anything. All we do is chomp on our food and it gets really a n n o y i n g. I'm starting to dread eating anything crispy. I wonder why they don't ask me questions. They really seem sad sometimes.

November 22nd, 1985

I was watching a cartoon in my room, Godzilla – The Magnetic Terror when I heard Henry and Tilda arguing from the kitchen. They talked so fast and they both had the accents that were hard to understand the words so I wasn't sure what they were fighting about. I didn't dare go out there. It lasted about five minutes and then I heard the front door slam. My bedroom faces the front so I sneaked a peek and watched Henry get in his car and drive away fast. I got a little scared. Could they be fighting about me? Did they not want me anymore? A little later Tilda knocked on my door and she came in and we talked. She finally started asking me questions. Questions about my parents. I told her more about my dad. When he was around he liked his leather chair and his fancy glass of whiskey or bourbon, I didn't know the difference. When he got home from trips, no matter what time of the day it was, he sat in that chair and had that drink and then he came to life. It was like a magical chair and a magic potion. Tilda told me they liked me very much and that we all needed to work hard to get to know each other so that we could understand each other.

November 25th, 1985

I started school. I actually got to go to a real school with real students and real teachers. The last time that happened was before I went to Chatterbee. Once I got to the orphanage I stopped going to school. We had a teacher that came to teach us on the property, but it just wasn't the same. Everyone seemed really cool. I looked all around for Adam. I thought maybe he went to the same school, but I didn't see him. I asked a couple kids if they knew him but they didn't. Tilda said Lady Henshaw never called her back with information on Adam. Maybe they weren't allowed to give that information out.

Or maybe Henshaw was being her normal bitch of a self.

November 30th, 1985

My first week of school was a winner, I think. I did get in a fight in the bathroom with some prick who was calling me Little Orphan Annie. I'm not sure how the jerk knew that I was an orphan. The only kid I told was Macie, a cute girl I sit next to in three classes and we sort of like each other, I think. But I asked her not to say anything. Anyhow, I gave the asshole a bloody nose, but he started it. I didn't get called to the office, so he must have cleaned up and didn't tell anyone he got his ass kicked. Ha ha ha. Dinner, Dinner! Henry and Tilda took me out to eat to celebrate my first week of school. We went to an Italian place called Marruccio's. I was slurping up a spaghetti noodle when a couple stopped by our table. Seemed they knew my fake parents and they wondered who this boy was (me) who was slurping his noodles with them. They told them my name, and that was it. Nothing like, this is our fake son, or we bought the boy from Henshaw, or this fine young man is a new addition to our family. Just Martin. This is Martin. I think I'm getting ahead of myself. It has only been a couple weeks. If I still called them fake parents why shouldn't they consider me just a boy who is staying with them?

December 2nd, 1985

We had a very nice weekend. We went to a museum yesterday and then out to eat again. Today I helped Tilda make a vegetable soup. I cut up vegetables for her. Henry didn't help do anything. I have noticed he doesn't help in the kitchen. He will clear the table after dinner but that is about all. I now have a chore schedule, which is fine. We had chores at Chatterbee and I am used to that, so it is no biggie. So far, I really think this is working out good. I am trying extra, extra, extra hard to make them happy — to do what is expected of me and to not talk back. Henry actually had a talk with me yesterday morning while Tilda was at the market. We sat at the dinner table and he asked about my hobbies and interests and he wanted to know how school was going. I told him I got into a fight. He thought that was great, which kind of surprised me. He told me: Don't take anyone's shit, Martin. Kids can be cruel when they find out you are different or come from a background that is different from their's. You stand up to them, show them you are the boss and what they are saying or doing is wrong. I used to get bullied when I was a kid. All the time. I was too scared to stand up for myself and it made me scared to go to school every day. I would tell my mum and dad I was sick all the time to get out of being picked on. I don't want that for you, okay? I was so excited. At Chatterbee we didn't get fed or kids visited the crate when we got in fights. It was not acceptable to fight. But here it is okay. I am not going to be scared to punch someone out if they're being a wanker idiot. This talk with Henry made me feel good about how our friendship was going. Before that he never really said a lot. It was mostly Tilda doing all the parenting stuff.

December 7th, 1985

Another week of school went good. I think everyone knows I'm adopted. I feel like they're all looking at me. I hear comments but no one has gotten in my face like the other guy. Macie said she never told anyone. I'm not sure I believe her. But I still like her. Macie talked me into trying out for the school play, Arsenic and Old Lace. That was the first time I ever did anything like that. It was a wee bit stressful. I counted twenty-two other kids auditioning. We had to stand on the stage and read with everyone watching. They will post a cast list next week sometime. I would be very surprised and very terrified if I got a role.

December 11th, 1985

Henry asked me to help him bring boxes up from the basement. I got the shivers going down there. It was dark and cold and was probably just like the basement at Chatterbee. The walls of the basement were rocks and you had to duck to not hit your head on the ceiling. Well, he had to duck, I mean. I wasn't yet tall enough to worry about it. But I couldn't get the thought of being locked in a crate and the stories I had heard out of my head. The boxes we brought up had Christmas stuff in them. And I helped decorate the house and put up a tree and decorate the tree. It was the most fun I've had in a while. The last time I decorated for Christmas was when my mum and dad were still alive. I was eight years old. We never did it together as a family like here. My dad was never around, so it was mostly just my mum and me. It was still always fun. I loved how the dark and dreary winter turned bright and jolly with the lights and the shiny red, green and gold decorations.

December 16th, 1985

I got a role in the play!

Really can't believe it! It's not a big role, I play a cop or something. We start rehearsing after school when we get back from Christmas break. I told Henry and Tilda and they were happy. Tilda more so than Henry. Henry asked if there were any sports I might be interested in as well. Tilda gave him a stern look. I told him I liked soccer. We played soccer a bunch at Chatterbee. I told him I would look into trying out for the team. That made him happy. Macie got one of the lead roles. She is so smart and funny and pretty. I really can't wait to spend more time with her after school. I am a little worried about Dylan, though. He's the guy I punched in the nose. I see them talking at her locker sometimes. She says he's just a friend. And she has never mentioned me punching him, so I don't think he told anyone. He stays away from me. And I don't have any classes with him, so that's good.

December 20th, 1985

Henry and Tilda took me to the shopping centre and set me free with enough coin to buy each of them something nice for Xmas.

I got Henry a watch with a gold band and I got Tilda a set of pots and pans. Sounds rubbish but that's what she wanted. We stopped and had some hot cocoa at a little booth on the way out.

And then the most amazing thing happened — I saw <u>ADAM</u>!

We hugged and I got to meet his adoptive parents. They seemed nice. We exchanged phone numbers and I told him I would call him the weekend after Christmas. It had been a year since he left Chatterbee and he grew a couple inches. He was getting as tall as me!

I can't wait to ask him a bunch more. Like, are his folks as great as mine?

Christmas Day, 1985!

Christmases at Chatterbee were exciting the first couple of years, but I was ten the first year and still believed. I still had hope, I suppose. And then the people that took care of us stopped doing nice things and we only got a gift or two each and they usually weren't the gifts we wanted. My buddy, Marie, the cleaning lady always gave me something extra, but she had to sneak it to me so she didn't get in trouble for showing me favoritism. I am happy to say I have found that excitement again, and it is all thanks to the Evans! Henry and Tilda and me had such a great day with the gifts (I got a hunting knife! And Henry showed me how to carve the turkey with it!) I also got some card games, an electronic football game and of course socks and underwear and this really cool neon green knapsack. They really liked the gifts I got them, too. We had cookies and milk and sat all morning playing with our stuff.

December 27th, 1985

I called and talked to Adam. We talked on the phone for an hour. He told me every-thing he has been doing and he talked about his new family. He has two older sisters and a younger brother. I can tell he doesn't like his fake brothers and sisters, at least not all of them. He didn't have a lot to say about the one sister, but he didn't explain and I guessed it was because he had people all around him when he was trying to talk. I was also sitting in the dining ~~room and~~ couldn't talk in private. I did not have my own phone in my room. We couldn't talk about how crazy it was at Chatterbee. About how horrible Henshaw was and about all the bad stuff that happened. How we could have died in the trash con-tainer. We couldn't let anyone know about the bad stuff because we might end up back there if our new family reported the stuff to the police. Adam and me will always have that connection and one day when we're older we can talk about it again.

January 6th, 1986

Back to school and I have to say I am happy for that. It seems I am in a boring space with Henry and Tilda. We just sit and eat or sit and watch dumb sitcoms or walk around the park. It is becoming a little too much like a habit, the things we do. We have meatloaf every Wednesday and seafood on Fridays. Every morning a three-egg omelet is waiting for me when I step out of my room. A slice of toast with cinnamon butter and a big glass of milk, too. I still hear walking outside my door a couple nights a week and I am almost ready to ask what that is all about, but not just yet. I am very scarce with my questions. I don't want to get on their nerves.

January 10th, 1986
Fight Part 2

We had three rehearsals after school for Arsenic and Old Lace this week. I was a little scared about it but Macie was very nice to me. She kept me calm and gave me some tips on how to act so it didn't look like I was acting. I started feeling closer to her, She touched my arm about five times during my scenes. **AND THEN IT HAPPENED AGAIN** Dylan showed up and started calling me Annie again. He told me Macie was his girlfriend and to stay away from her. And then he called me other names like fag, retard and loser. I asked him if he wanted more of what I gave him a couple months ago and he kicked me in the shin. When I fell down he jumped me and started punching me in the back of my head. We were in the back of the auditorium while rehearsal

for a scene I wasn't in was happening on stage but it was kinda dark and they couldn't see but they could hear. I was able to throw him off me and then I went to town on the asshole. I beat the holy snot out of him. I kept thinking what Henry told me, to stand up for myself. To never let anyone treat me like dirt. When everyone got to the back of the auditorium they saw a bloody Dylan. And bloody me. I had his blood all over me. I thought the blood came mostly from his nose but I saw some running down his ear, too. I was taken to the Principal's office and they called Tilda to pick me up. She seemed mad at me, but I explained to her what happened and what Henry told me to do and then she said I was wrong and he was wrong.

January 11th, 1986

I was suspended from school and kicked off the play. Tilda cried when she told me. Henry didn't say a word to me. I was grounded which wasn't fair. I was doing what I was told to do. I was very confused. Henry wouldn't tell me I did a good job. And then I found out Dylan's in the hospital. They think he could lose his hearing in one of his ears. I feel terrible. I never wanted it to go that far, but once I started punching I couldn't stop. It all happened so fast.

January 12th, 1986

Cops showed up and took us all to the
station We were there all day,
Dylan's parents were pressing charges
against Henry and me. More
Henry because he told me to do it. I made
the mistake of saying that to the Principal
the day it happened. I am not allowed to
go back to Henry and Tilda's house.
The police have called for someone to
pick me up. I have no idea who it will be.

January 13th, 1986

THE <u>WORST DAY OF MY LIFE</u>!!

I'm back at Chatterbee.
I've lost my new parents, who were no longer my fake parents. They packed my knapsack with a few clothing items for my return to hell. I had to go to Henshaw's office when I got there and she went crazy on me.

She said stuff like:
You are an embarrassment to this organization. Do you understand how this makes us look? You will never have another opportunity like that one. Nobody will ever want you. You will rot in this place.

And then I was taken to the basement.

CHAPTER TWELVE: CRATE TRAINING

January 14th, 1986
My Worst Fears

The place I always feared.

The dark I never wanted to enter.

The anger I didn't want to feel.

That moment arrived last night.

I was escorted down the stairs by two security guards, or cooks, or maintenance guys, who knew what they did as all the workers had many jobs. How could these two guys think this was okay? Why wouldn't they try to stop this abuse? Made me sick to my belly. I didn't fight it. What was the point.

IT WAS A BLOODY DOG CRATE!

I got on my hands and knees and crawled into the crate. I wasn't convinced the stories were true, that it was an actual crate for a dog. The only good discovery was that it was larger. It looked like it could house a golden retriever. A solid metal tray lined the bottom, so that helped. At least I wasn't touching the cement floor. But it was still cold.

I got a good look around the basement before they went back up the stairs and turned off the lights. The crate was screwed to the wall so I couldn't try to roll it around and break out that way. The little door I crawled in was pad locked, so that couldn't be broken with my bare hands. The gaps in the crate were big enough to squeeze my hand out but the metal was thick. I tried kicking the side and it didn't give. It didn't bend. I could sit and the top of my head touched the top of the crate, so there was more room than I guessed. I curled into a ball and closed my eyes. The black didn't get blacker, though. I thought about the last couple months. I thought about my freedom and how great it was but also how hard it was to be in a home with strangers pretending to be my dead parents. Being out in the real world again and trying to function as a regular boy after being in this rubbish prison for the last four years was really hard. But the thought of being stuck at Chatterbee until I was a legal adult was scarier than the dark. Four more years. No way in bloody fucking hell was that gonna happen. I would plan another escape. I would find a new guy or two to help me.

I miss Adam even more now. I want to talk to him. I wonder if he knows what happened to me. *MY KNAPSACK, BLANKET AND FLASHLIGHT!* I had just fallen asleep, not sure how, very tired I guess, when the light came on and I heard footsteps coming down the old wooden stairs. The basement was as huge as the building was, the size of a mansion. Not sure what to compare it to. The Playboy Mansion? I saw that on TV once. That old man and all those boobies. Maybe I could picture myself living there. And then a vision of Lady Henshaw in a bikini came to my mind and I wanted to vomit. Not sure how a large pear would even fit into a bikini and that sour face, just no. No!!!! I figured it was her coming down the stairs to yell at me some more. But it wasn't Henshaw. It was MARIE! And she had a blanket and a flashlight and my knapsack which had this journal in it, so I could write all of this while locked up. She shoved it all through the larger gap in the front. The gap where they shoved the food in, I would think, if I'm to be fed. Marie spoke quietly: I'm so sorry she's doing this to you, but it will be okay. It will only be until morning and you can keep warm and stay lit down here.

The place has been treated for vermin so you shouldn't see any rats or spiders or anything like that. Marie sat on the floor next to me and we talked for a while. She said Henshaw had to leave for a bit so she wasn't worried about getting caught down here. I told her about Henry and Tilda and the good times. About the fight with Dylan that put me back here. I wanted to keep talking and talking but she had to get back upstairs. I asked her one last question: Why did she stay at Chatterbee? Why would she work for someone like Henshaw and why wouldn't she report her for the bad things she did? (Okay, it was more like three last questions.) She told me: 'm old and not in great health. Lady Henshaw is very good to me. She helps me pay for my doctor's bills and allows me to stay here. I have no other family. If I reported her and turned on her she would throw me out on the street. But trust me, if she ever did anything to put you kids in danger I would put my foot down. I would draw a line and take my chances. She told me she would sneak back down before morning to collect my things and away she went. I'M LIVE — LIVE ON THE AIR I'm going live right now. I am writing as I'm curled up in the crate.

The little flashlight next to me is helping me see. I'm not sure I agreed with Marie about us not being in danger, about her stepping up if we were in danger. Yeah, Henshaw never held a gun to our heads, but she did mess with our heads. She hurt our heads with her words. Her insults. Couldn't words be just as dangerous as physical actions? I hear a noise coming from the other end of the basement and I shine my flashlight. The brick walls bounce the light around but the little flashlight isn't strong enough to go the entire length of the dungeon. I keep it pointed in the direction of the sound, waiting to catch the eyes of some creature. A cellar dwelling reptile with red, glowing eyes and razor sharp teeth and walks with a limp. A monster that walks on all fours but can also walk on its back legs and is as tall as the ceiling when he stands straight. He will come to visit my new home and rip the door off before pulling me out and ripping me apart. First my right arm, then my left leg, then he'll start with my pointer finger on my left hand and maybe a toe or two from my right foot. Before I bleed to death he'll use both of his sharp claws to scoop my head right off my shoulders and throw it down the basement like a bowling ball. Maybe he'll have bones of his past victims standing up down there, like bowling pins.

I THINK I WATCHED TOO MANY SCARY MOVIES AT HENRY AND TILDA'S HOUSE.

I can't believe I won't get to stay in that bedroom with the TV ever again. Henry will be blamed for making me a lunatic and he will be unfit to ever be allowed to adopt again. Will I ever see Macie again? Should I even care? This whole thing could be her fault. If she hadn't told Dylan I was adopted - if she hadn't flirted with me when she was supposedly his girlfriend. Screw that girl. What is that? Another movement from the shadows. This time it is obvious. Something is walking towards me. I'm keeping the light pointed that way waiting to see what will emerge. Marie said no vermin. Glowing eyes! Not red, though, more blue-ish. And then the body is exposed. A slight whine comes out of it's mouth as it moves closer. Oh my god. It is a dog. A medium sized black and tan dog with floppy ears and a long nose. His fur is longer and seems matted in places. How did he get in? I wonder where he came from. I say hello and he comes to my cage. How weird is it I am locked in the dog crate and he is standing outside of it. I laugh a little bit at the absurdity.

He has a collar on and I am able to reach it and see a tag with the name BOW on it. He is a nice dog. I talk to him and ask him to stay. He plops down on the cement next to my shelter and sighs and then falls asleep. His breathing is deep and groggy. It seems he may be an older pooch. I've never seen Bow on the grounds before, but I have been gone. He could be a new addition. I reach my hand out from the bottom of the crate and I grab his paw. I hold onto it as I lay there and tell him all about my life until I fall asleep.

January 15th, 1986

Henshaw never came down to get me out of the cage, it was the two brutes from the night before. Marie came before them and gathered my things in the morning and told me Henshaw rarely comes down to the basement. She told me Bow was new and that he lives in the basement. There is a broken window he comes in and out of. Henshaw fought to have Bow removed but agreed to allow him to stay as long as he stayed out of her way. The staff was in charge of buying the food and taking care of him. He was only allowed in the basement-not inside anywhere else. I'm now back in my old room with my old roomie that nobody seems to want, either. Brandon. He tells me: I really missed you, Martin. Things haven't been the same since you left. I almost had a welcoming family but they chose Max instead. I met a girl and we kissed. We had a little affair. But she's gone. I don't really like the new kids, none of them are like you, Martin. You just get me. I can be myself around you. I think it's because we have been roommates for so long, etc. etc. Two minutes back in the room and I wanted to scream. But I also agreed about there being a comfort with Brandon. More of a familiarity, I suppose.

January 20th, 1986

Back to the classes at Chatterbee.
No more school, no more lockers, no more
trying out for plays and sports and coming
home to vegetable soup and ham and cheese
sandwiches. I had a meeting with Henshaw
yesterday and she lashed out at me again.
I don't care what your story was, Martin.
You're a known liar, so I don't believe your
adoptive father made you beat anyone up.
He surely didn't tell you to put the boy in
the hospital. I don't care if that wasn't your
intention. This incident goes in your file and
will be presented to any couple interested in
adopting you. Their interest will turn to
disinterest when they hear of this horrible
affair. I wondered what was actually in my
file. When she said file I looked behind her
and saw a filing cabinet. Two of them,
actually. Eight drawers total. I was in one of
them. I needed to see my file. There had to
be a reason so few couples ever interviewed
me in the four years.

I had a new goal — a new purpose:

Get in that cabinet and get my file!

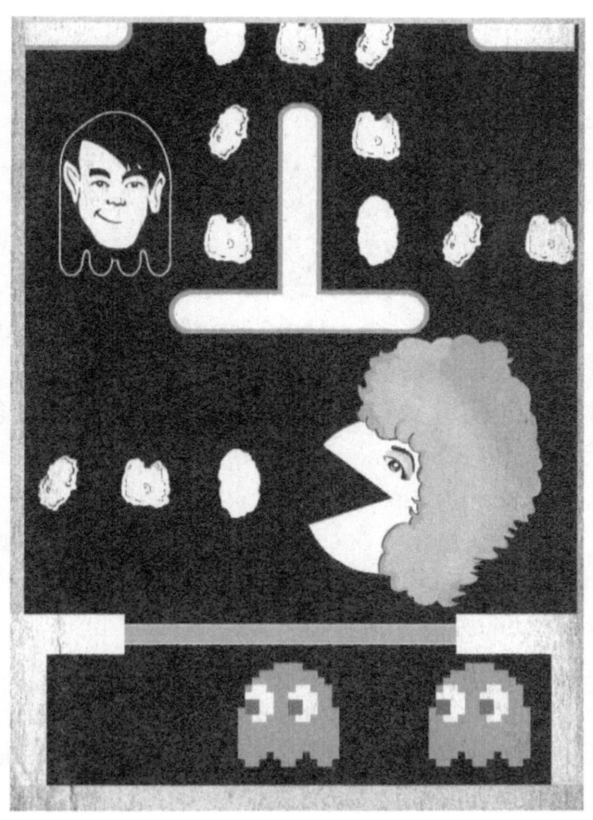

CHAPTER THIRTEEN: SIBLING REVELRY

Digging into the neon knapsack revived Martin's story even though the saga was always stored in my brain and was a simple trigger away. He was just as important now as he was then but I needed to continue packing the house after completing my first meaningful AA meeting in Sundown. Baby Beans dolls stared at me as I removed the twins from an unmarked box.

My brother pulled in the driveway, finally arriving. The sibling disconnection we had as kids passed into adulthood. He lived at home until age thirty and instead of college he worked in manufacturing warehouses moving products around with forklifts. The allure of Nashville and creating music eventually led to his move to The Music City where he played gigs on the main drag a couple times a month. He never married or had kids and I realized he was an introvert who preferred limited time around other people. He enjoyed quality time with himself creating music.

"Lamie Mamie put me to shamie," Theo said as he closed the car door and I wished the rhyme had died but as he neared age fifty my brother still thought it was funny. Never did I laugh and it seemingly became a personal attack as I attached it to my struggles with addiction. I always felt like a lamie for being unable to control my alcohol urges.

"Just in time," I said and reached my arms around his tall, skinny body. We always hugged; it was comforting if only for a moment. The last time I saw him was at our dad's funeral. He was closer to home and was around more to help our folks as they ailed and I was grateful. "I ordered a dumpster, now all we need is a backhoe excavator," I joked.

"Boxing this stuff up was the greatest thing since sliced bread," he said as he adjusted his plaid, newsboy hat on his bald head.

"Anything you remember? Most of these boxes aren't labeled," I said, jabbing at his tendency to half-ass assignments. "Oh, did you ever get a gay vibe from dad?"

"Ummm, huh?"

"Remember Chuck? Chuck was in love with dad. I found a letter." I told the trout story as Theo stared and thought hard to remember moments.

"Maybe he was bisexual. Or pansexual. Or omnisexual. Or demisexual."

"Okay, of those four I only know what bisexuality is. Back in the day you were gay or straight. What the hell is demisexual? Being attracted to Demi Moore? If that's the case then I'm probably demisexual."

"Google it. I don't have all day to explain."

"So, are you attracted to Demi Moore? Or pans – is that what pansexual is? Do you get it on with your nonstick cookware?" I asked and giggled but really was curious why he was never in a committed relationship, or even a casual relationship. Was he attracted to pans? "You can tell me anything, you know. Is there anyone special in your life? You're a great-looking man, surely, you're rolling in the hay?"

He stopped rummaging and stared at me. "Are we really going to have this conversation? Sex is gross, okay, I don't do it."

"Wait, you never did it? Ever?"

"I did do it," he sighed and shook his head. "Okay, you already have that judgy tone about you. Yes, I tried it, both ways, all ways. I had to determine what I was attracted to and it turns out I am not attracted to anything."

"I understand. Wait, is there a word for that?"

"Asexual. Why didn't you ever ask me that before? Nobody ever asked me. Not even mom or dad."

"We were waiting for you to figure it out. Didn't want to force you to come out if you were gay," I said, mentally noting to Google asexuality later; just because sexual attraction didn't exist, couldn't emotional attraction? Relationships existed without the sex, just ask married couples after five years. If a life of solitude worked for Theo, I was happy for him and would stop thinking about fixing him up with every weird single woman I knew.

Theo continued to poke around, not asking anything more about Chuck and dad, or sex, and grabbed a marker and labeled a couple boxes.

"So, did you tell Abigail and Lucas yet? We kept our promise to mom that we wouldn't tell anyone until they were both gone. At least I kept my promise," Theo said, ready to move on from the awkward sexual interrogation. He jumped to a topic far more controversial and it was my turn to be interrogated.

"No. I haven't told the kids. I'm not sure there is much of a reason to now, right?"

"What do you mean, Mamie? Don't you think getting it out in the open will be therapeutic for you? Haven't you struggled with this most of your life? And what about your drinking? Hasn't it been a trigger for getting loaded?"

"Loaded? C'mon Theo, I'm not a baked potato."

Theo unstacked a couple boxes and placed a bigger box on the corner of a dust covered antique desk and opened the lid. "This is his stuff, Mamie. Is Abigail here now? I can help you through this. I am here to support you."

I'm not sure Theo had ever offered to support me and I was touched. I bit my lower lip as my eyes watered. I looked in the box and pulled out the red electronic game that looked like a phone and the cheesy, 80's commercial rang in my ears:

Merlin's a game that you can play, you can play it six different ways. Merlin's a game that's lots of fun...

"Will you please turn off that game. It's cleaning day. Time to straighten up your bedroom, Theo," my mom said as he sat in front of the television set like a zombie, playing Atari. I didn't understand how he kept his cool while battling aliens or avoiding ghosts. Anytime I lost a life in one of the dozen games we owned I screamed and tossed the joystick. Ms. Pacman was my biggest trigger. Her gobbling drove me over the edge.

My mom looked at me as I finished my bowl of Honey Bunches of Oats cereal. It was Sunday morning, two days after my stolen innocence and four days after the fatal plane explosion. My mom finally had a day off work and I fully expected her to question me about the last few days. My dad wasn't home to protect me.

"How many bowls of that sugar do you plan on eating? It'll be lunch time soon," she said to me, once again using her words as weapons. The only days I dodged criticisms for my eating habits were days she worked. Once I tried to make her pay by going on a hunger strike for two days. She laughed at me and told me if I pulled it off, she'd fill a baby pool with Little Debbie snacks and let me swim through them and eat as many as I wanted. The strike lasted three hours. I got busted with a Pixy Stix, which was freakin flavored powder—not food. We fought over it and I decided to shove a handful of peanut M&Ms down my throat to shut us both up.

"Yeah, this is the last bowl of sugar, mom. Then I plan to eat a bowl of salt. And then pepper. Or maybe I'll mix the salt and pepper and sprinkle in a pinch of cyanide. Then when I'm regurgitating my cereal all over the kitchen you can scoop the nuggets back up, run them under some cold water and repackage them for Theo. Not for me because I'll be dead," I said as I dumped the remaining milk and cereal into the sink. I was a bitchy kid, but she made me that way. If she wasn't riding my ass in constant disapproval, I'd be Susie Sunshine.

"Are you trying out for the school play next year? You have that dramatic thing down pretty well," she said, not getting too upset that morning. "Now, Mamie, I-"

"Yes, I know, mom. I'm heading to my room to clean, too," I said, stopping another nagging comment in its tracks.

"Okay. Yes. But I wanted to talk to you, first."

I stopped on the way to my room. Theo's eyes were glued to the UFOs he blasted as I tried to make eye contact with him, concerned he opened his big mouth about the neon bag hiding in my closet.

"What do you want to talk about?" I asked, taking a big breath.

"What happened to you on Wednesday?"

"What do you mean?"

"Your head. And your knees. You fell on the way to school?

"Yes. I tripped."

"You were exactly under the plane explosion, Mamie. I know when you left, I knew where you were. I called the school to make sure you were there and not splattered on the path to the school. You are lucky you weren't hit with anything."

"Yeah." I didn't share the severed hand attack.

"I guess I'm confused why you wouldn't be talking about it. Why you wouldn't be making a big dramatic statement with it, or bragging about having seen it?"

Theo was expressionless. He was unreadable, but if he wasn't the exploding time bomb, he had to be hoping I spilled the beans so he didn't have to keep the secret from his mommy. I had to be as clever as Devisha and come up with an amazing work of fiction.

"I was scared. I mean, I'm scarred from this. I think I might have that post pardon trauma thing, mom," I said, confident I made Devisha proud.

"Post pardon is when you're depressed after having a baby. Post-traumatic stress disorder is what I think you were trying to say, which is laughable," Theo said. I hated him.

"Why don't you shut your face, Theo, and mind your own business. I'm allowed to have stress disorder. I mean, five people died right above my head. I probably had blood on me from them, not just my own blood," I yelled at him, around a seven in volume. I turned back to my mom and she was no longer in the room. She had moved on to something else, like scrubbing the toilet bowl. I punched Theo in the shoulder and he almost lost a life in his game.

"Where did this come from?"

My mom appeared from the hallway with the neon green knapsack. And the time bomb had detonated after all. The look I gave Theo had to be terrifying. I've never wanted to murder someone until that day.

"Oh my god, mom! I don't have any privacy here!"

"Stop playing the victim, Mamie. You taking this bag from the accident site isn't nearly as bad as not telling anyone you took it. This is the property of someone who died. Don't you think their loved ones would want to have it?" Theo quit his game and excused himself to his room, saying he really needed to start cleaning. I wanted to jump the little snitch, but then I processed what my mother said about the loved ones wanting his stuff. I never thought about that aspect of it all.

"This bag belonged to a boy but he wasn't listed on the plane, mom. He wasn't one of the passengers. The news said there was a couple from Nashville, and two others from out-of-town going to a concert and the pilot. No mention of a boy. There's a journal in here and I've been reading it. I'm going to sort this out, mom. Just let me figure it out and we'll take it to the police."

"There are people still out there in those woods looking for evidence. If this bag was the only thing that wasn't destroyed it could lead them to answers."

"Let me get the answers, mom, okay? Please? Give me some more time," I pleaded as she turned and walked into the kitchen with the bag and placed it on the counter. "I need this, okay, I'm nothing. I'm worthless. I need something. Why can't this be my something. Theo has his straight As and your support and love and you're proud of him every single day. Maybe that's what I want, too. I want to make you proud."

"Your father and I are proud of you."

"Oh, you are? When? All I hear is how I eat too much, or the wrong food. I hear about how I dress like crap. I hear threats to be grounded because of my grades."

"Look, Mamie, I have to remind you to eat better. If I see you shove another twinkie down your throat I will lose my mind."

"That is exactly what I'm talking about! I'm on the verge of an eating disorder because of you, mom!" I kept pouring on the guilt. She was ready to cave, I was sure of it.

"I'm just looking out for your health. All around. Your physical and mental health, Mamie. If you're overweight, you get bullied and your classmates won't take you seriously. They won't be your friends. That will be tough, mentally." I understood that point, but surely there was a better way to approach me about that, and other areas of improvement. "Okay, look. What is it you need to do with this stuff?" she motioned to the bag.

"It's the journal. I'm almost done reading it. This poor kid was adopted and then returned to the orphanage, but something isn't right. He's about to break into this lady's office to look at his file."

"I'll allow you to continue on one condition. You let me help you. We figure this out together," she said, much to my surprise. My initial reaction was to whine about not doing it myself. I wanted the glory and the recognition. I was the one who survived the shards of metal flying overhead and I was the one who risked my life to get the bag out of the tree. I shouldn't be required to share the achievement. But after a moment I decided it was okay. I realized my mother actually wanted to spend time with me. She wanted to help me uncover the truth about the boy and that was a great way to bond with her. Oh, and I wouldn't get grounded if she helped. That was also an important point.

She handed me the knapsack and asked me to empty it. We looked at the items spread out on the sofa. The hunting knife was still stained with dried blood. She sorted through the other items with little interest. I held the journal up and shared the stories of the Escape Club and The Crate and The Evans and my mother listened with interest. Theo came out of his room and sat with us and I wanted to be mad but it might turn out okay after all. His act of betrayal might just get me the attention I desperately wanted. My mom asked me to read the journal and I pulled it open to the page with the folded corner and continued to read, this time aloud.

January 25th, 1986

Life in Chatterbee is back to basics. There are a few new faces but I can't approach them just yet with an escape plan. I will study them and decide who could be my next bestie. I need to figure out who is the most desperate, first. Speaking of besties, I needed to call Adam. I did have his number written down, but the only phones were in the main office and you needed approval to use them and then people listen. Henshaw's office was right off the main office. I still needed to find a way in there to get into my file.

January 26th, 1986

It's Sunday and the staff is limited. Henshaw is usually not here either. Marie is here and I asked her to help me get into my file. She was very scared about that. She didn't know if there was a spare key to get into Henshaw's office. When she cleaned the office it was during the week and she worked around Henshaw or Henshaw stepped out for a few minutes while she swept the area carpet or wiped down her desk. Marie said she would try to get into the file cabinet her next cleaning. I also asked her if I could call Adam and she took me to the offices and let me use the phone. **HE ANSWERED ON THE SECOND RING!!** We talked for half an hour. He couldn't believe I was back at the orphanage. He said he would come to visit me. I wrote down his address and asked him if I could stay with him if I escaped. Marie looked at me and shook her head NO. NO she did not want me to escape. But what she didn't know wouldn't hurt her, right? I would plan this without her knowing. I told Adam I couldn't wait to see him again and we said goodbye. And then I asked Marie if I could call Henry and Tilda. She said stuff like: No. Absolutely not. You are not allowed to talk to them. Do you not understand the severity of what you've done? You are lucky to be back here and not some juvenile detention center, Martin. You need to tread very lightly. No escape plan. I will try to see your file but if there isn't an opportunity I cannot risk getting caught! She took me back to my room and to my obnoxious roommate who was amped up on Mountain Dew or something. He was jumping up and down on his bed singing that Humpty Dumpty song. I escaped by crawling under my blankets to play with Merlin. And no I didn't name my willy Merlin. Haha.

Drops of Water

Drip, drip, drip goes the spicket.
Swish, swish, swish goes the water
down into darkness
A darkness a human soul cannot know
A place you don't want to go
Where life is crazy and happiness
is missing
Where your thoughts are black
and your voice is not heard
Where you can be attacked for existing
and destroyed with a flip of a switch
You could be defeated by rotten lettuce
or the fat from a ribeye steak
The disposal blades chop a lot
and keeps the bad food from hitting the pot
But then it rains into your head as you
try to flee the dark
The depressed need to emerge into light
And the drip, drip, dries in sight.

March 1st 1986

Nothing has happened in a month. Nothing exciting and I'm boring myself. Marie didn't come through with my file. She claims Henshaw is always there and the cabinet is locked so it would be nearly impossible to get in there. I love Marie, but I think she is full of shit. Adam hasn't been over to visit and nobody answers the phone when I try to call. I have a bad feeling his fake mommy and daddy killed our friendship. I'm sure it's because of what I did to that asshole boy in school. I keep going over everything that happened and I feel so sick that I almost had everything I wanted but threw it all away to please a man trying to be my father. I threw it all away trying to build a relationship with a man I never ever had in my life. I didn't have it with my real dad and my fake dad was the last ditch effort. Now I would never know how it felt to have a father who was proud of me. I wouldn't know how it felt to be a good son. Who was in my life that I cared to please or make proud? Maybe Marie, but lately it seems she's been distant.

NO INTERVIEWS

Nobody cared to see me. Nobody wants to adopt a problem boy. Henshaw will see that I'm stuck here until I'm legal. She's evil, I'm convinced of it. She is bitter and spiteful. If someone else a lot more understanding was running Chatterbee I would have been long gone. I really hate the woman. I have no connection to any new boys and it seems the number of kids at Chatterbee was at an all-time low. Brandon was adopted last week and I think I actually miss the asshole. My room is too quiet now. I do have BOW. Bow WoW! I visit with him outside every day. I take him scraps of food after lunch every day and we sit against the building and talk about life. He tells me about his previous owner and how he took up a home at Chatterbee. He was like one of us, a being needing adopted. He needed a family just as bad as me, but maybe together we could be each other's family. My plan was to take him with me if I was ever plucked from Chatterbee. It would be more like ChatterBEEN!

I garnered the attention of everyone in the room. My voice was perfect for reading this story and I might have a future as an audio book narrator.

"Why are you reading in order? You want the answer to why this guy was flying to Tennessee, just turn to the last couple pages," Theo correctly suggested. Days could've been saved to skip to the end, but then it would be like watching a murder mystery on VHS tape and fast forwarding to the identity of the killer. It lacked suspense. It lacked true connection and heart. It would be soulless. "Let me have it. I'll skip to the end but I won't tell you how it ends or why it ends," he reached for the journal in my hands but I pulled it away from him.

"No!"

"Theo, stop," my mom said. "We're going to finish it today. By the end of the day all of our questions will be answered."

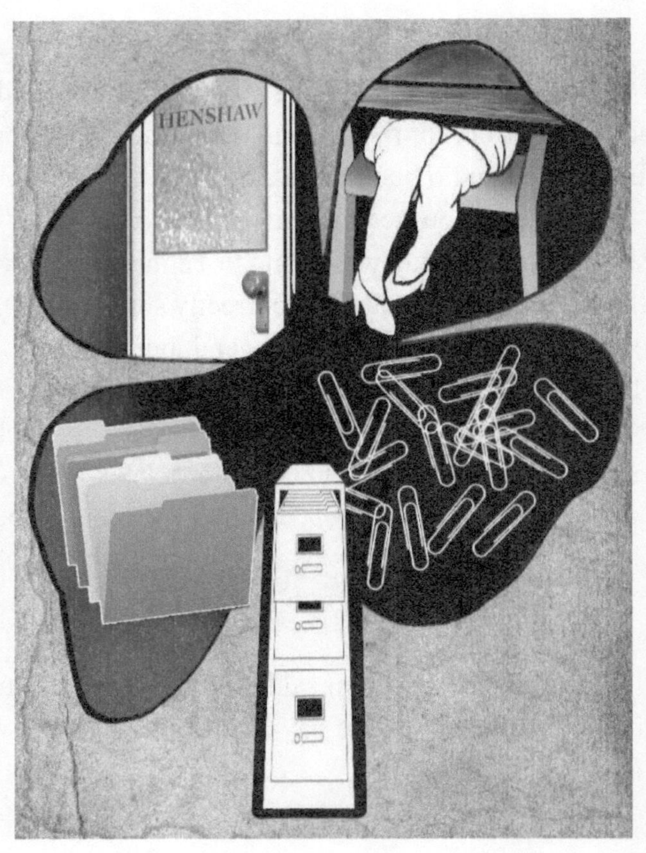

CHAPTER FOURTEEN: GRAND LUNACY

"Hello my little Blackheads. Who needs a good popping?"

My dad flew in the door with his energy and his smile and his lunacy. The zit-popping joke associated with our unfortunate name wore out its welcome many years ago. Actually, it was never welcomed, although he continued to squeeze puss out of it.

And us.

He nearly lost an eye from a wart or goiter or something he squeezed on Theo's back. I walked in the room as that happened. I nearly blew chunks.

"What is happening? You playing cards or something? Isn't it cleaning day?"

Theo explained to my dad what was happening and he wasn't upset or puzzled about me having the knapsack or the journal, which proved my brother blabbed to my dad before he told my mother. I'm surprised my trader brother never turned me in for my pot smoking. And thank God he didn't know what happened to me at the party the other night. My mother would not be as forgiving with that information.

My dad grabbed a soda and plopped on the sofa between Theo and my mom and the three of them stared at me, waiting for my award-winning narration to continue. The atmosphere had the feel of a campfire and I was telling the scary story of the evil Lady Henshaw and the perils at Chatterbee Orphanage. I was the lead actress on an illuminated stage, captivating my audience. My mother was stepping outside of her comfort zone and being nice and giving me the attention I craved. As the page count dwindled, I would read slowly and more dramatically, savoring every minute I was in the spotlight.

"Okay, Mamie. Get moving, we have to get back to cleaning," my mom ordered, returning to her comfort zone.

March 17th, 1986
St. Paddys Day

Henshaw decided to celebrate St. Patrick's Day this year. The staff decorated the cafeteria in green and white streamers and balloons. We had classes in the morning and then after lunch we were to hang in the cafeteria. I thought maybe today could be the day I try to grab my file. Maybe Henshaw would be distracted with the party and leave something unlocked. We had lunch first. I sat with Randolph and Jack. They were newer victims and Jack had already spent a night in the crate for talking back to the queen. He said it was the best night of sleep he's had in awhile. He was a beast. I needed him on my team, but I couldn't scheme with him with Randolph around. Randolph was several years younger and messed up in the noggin. He was extremely emotional and nervous about everything. So, I had to wait until after we ate and then I cornered Jack. I was only going to talk about an escape plan but then I thought he could help me get my file.

I'm all you, bloke. This place is rotten and I smell it in the walls. It smells like decay. I'm not staying here. He was out there, but he was strong-willed. Nobody would want him. He was sixteen, though, so he'd be out in a couple years, except he didn't want to wait a couple years. I convinced him I needed to see my file first and then we would work on an escape plan. Henshaw was at the food line talking to one of the staff members. I told Jack to keep an eye on her and distract her if she leaves before I get back. He said easy, peasy and off I went to her office. I made sure the rest of the office staff were in the cafeteria. They were all sitting together, away from the kids. The main office was an open set up. There was a counter in the middle where guests would approach and then there were a handful of private offices lining the right and the left sides. Separate doors for each office. Henshaw's office was in the back right corner. You had to get beyond the counter, which stretched from right wall to left wall. Since nobody was there I pushed open the little half door and walked fast to Henshaw's door, which was

closed. It wasn't until I got there and grabbed
the handle that I found out it was unlocked.
I WAS IN!!!
I went straight to the cabinets and they were
both locked. I went to her desk to find a key.
I pulled open the little drawers on
top but couldn't find keys. They seemed like
junk drawers. Lipstick and fingernail files and
rubber bands and paperclips. PAPERCLIPS!
I grabbed a couple of them and unbent them,
I saw this in movies. I put both ends into the
lock and moved them around,
thinking the drawer would immediately pop
open. It didn't.
AGAIN — AGAIN — AGAIN —
AGAIN — **AGAIN**
Nothing. I really sucked at this and
I wondered if it was even
possible. The movies were full of shit.
SHIT I tell you!
And
Then
it
opened.
But there weren't any files on the kids in any
of the four drawers of the cabinet I unlocked.

So I moved over to the other cabinet. As I was shoving the paper clips in that lock I heard footsteps coming from outside the door. I had closed Henshaw's door as to not attract attention, and to hide myself, obviously. I panicked and crawled under the desk. The front was solid so I would not be seen. All I could hope was it wasn't Henshaw and she didn't sit at her desk. The thought of her crotch sliding into my face had me vomiting in my mouth a little. I pulled the chair on wheels back into the desk to seal me in. And then the door opened and the footsteps, high heel shoes, walked into the office. Henshaw loved her high heels, so I was sure this was the queen. I didn't relock the cabinet I opened. Would she know? Then the chair was pulled away from me and although I was deep enough under the desk I felt exposed. Lady Henshaw! Lady Henshaw! Come quick! Before I was exposed to her smelly crotch she was summoned back to the cafeteria. Jack had worked his charms, it seemed.

I crawled out from under the desk and went to town on the second locked cabinet. After a few minutes it clicked open and I pulled each drawer open until I found the file named Martin Allen. It was pretty thick. And I hadn't thought about what I should do if I made it to this point. Do I take the entire file? How would I return it? Would she find it missing? What punishment would I face if I was caught? I suppose I should've thought about it more. I took the entire file folder, shoved the paper clips in my pocket and made sure everything was back the way it was. I didn't have time to relock the cabinets. I would have to hope she thought she left them open. But what if she was anal about keeping them locked? This would be a dead giveaway someone was in there and she would look for clues on who the culprit was which would lead her to my missing file. I emptied the documents onto her desk and stuck the hanging file folder with my name back in its proper slot. Then I grabbed the documents from another kid's folder and shoved them in mine to make it look as though nothing had been touched. This was a bloody brilliant decision.

If I had more time I would have patted myself on the back. I shoved the documents up the front of my shirt and carefully headed out of the offices and out into the hallway leading to the stairs.

MARIE!

She stepped out of the ladies room on the first floor and nearly bumped into me. I sucked my belly in and crossed my arms, holding the files in. I wasn't sure I could trust Marie anymore, since she hadn't helped me and became distant. She was the one who was supposed to get these files. Hi Martin! Are you having a good St, Patrick's Day? Are you leaving the party already? I told her the corned beef and cabbage did not agree with my stomach and continued my flight up the stairs and to my room. I DID IT! Now I needed to wait until night to inspect. Would my suspicions be confirmed? Had she been making up bad things about me to keep me at Chatterbee?

St. Paddys Day Part 2
♣ The Bloody File ♣

I waited until all was quiet that night and then I pulled the papers out from under my mattress. It seemed half the pages from my file was my recent adoption and police reports and bad stuff from the fight. Witness reports. Reports from Henry and Tilda. I read Henry's report first:

Martin insisted on handling things his own way, which usually led to violence. He has quite a bad temper. There were several times he got upset with us because we asked him to perform a chore or we asked him to stop playing with that bloody Merlin game and he would fly into a rage.

BULL SHIT! It was his writing, I recognized it from other documents I saw around their house. Nothing was fraudulent about this report except that what he was writing was complete bullshit! He was clearly trying to protect himself since I told people he suggested I beat the snot out of anyone that pushes me into a corner. I dug past other reports until I found Tilda's. I hoped she had my back, at least.

Martin is a lovely boy but very troubled. We feared approaching him because he had flown into rages. He once threw a pot across the kitchen because he lost at that Merlin game. When we tried to discipline him he went into a deep depression. We feared he may hurt himself or someone else.

Tilda used the fight she had in the kitchen with Henry that day but switched the characters around. I was now the bad guy. Clearly, the two of them had a talk about what they would say before speaking to authorities. This hurts, deep down, because somewhere in my mind I thought I might end up back with them. I thought after time had passed I would be allowed to try again with them. But now that wasn't going to happen. Henry and Tilda were officially dead to me. I lost another set of parents to death. I kept digging through the file. There were reviews of my behavior over the years.

I remember having meetings with mental health professionals. One doctor convinced me to document all my thoughts and feeling, that it would be helpful to me, which is why I write in this journal. BUT IS IT REALLY HELPFUL? DOES IT MAKE ONE OUNCE OF A FUCKING DIFFERENCE!!?? Like right now, I would say NO NO No! I actually feel like I'm more of a lunatic than ever before. And only adding to the feeling is coming across more reports about how I'm withdrawn from the other children — how I'm not friendly or inviting, how I don't include my former roommate Brandon in any of my playtime outings. Is this true? Am I really a douche bag? IS THERE ANYTHING GOOD ABOUT ME IN HERE!!?? I keep digging for a good report. Who in their right minds would look at these reports and want to welcome me into their home? I dig and dig and dig but nothing. SOMEONE KNOCKS ON MY DOOR! I freak out, shove everything into a pile and slid under my mattress again as the door opens. It is Marie. She's not dumb. She knows I took the files and she is in my room to get them back so she can try to return them without me getting caught. She apologies to me for not helping and she tells me she had just found out a week ago that her cancer had returned. I told her I never knew she had it to begin with. She told me not to worry myself about it, but wanted me to know that was why she didn't help me. She sits on my bed and we talk for a long time. I tell her about the bad reports and how my fake parents became legit fakers and I ask her if I'm as bad as the reports say. She hugs me and tells me I'm the sweetest boy that has ever come to Chatterbee. She tries to take the papers from me, but I won't let her. I tell her I don't want her to get caught and that I have a good plan to get them back safe and sound. Jack faked choking on sauerkraut earlier to get Henshaw out of the office. I imagine he'll choke on lettuce next time. Marie says she'll pray for me. I tell her I'll pray for her, too, even though that's not my thing. She also asks for me to consider her a parent. And NOT A FAKE PARENT. That she would have loved to have had a son like me. She leaves. I cry like a baby.

I think it was the hardest I've ever cried.

I'm sad I'll never have a mother because the mother I want will probably die from cancer.

I fell asleep with red eyes.

March 19th, 1986

I hadn't looked through anymore of my file since Monday. It was too depressing. I was ready to return it and accept the fact that I would be stuck at Chatterbee until I was 18. Unless I made an attempt to escape again. I talked to Jack about it. I told him about the previous escape plan and how it turned deadly. He said we were dumb idiots and he laughed. He said we didn't need to jump inside the trash container to get out with the trash truck. We could simply jump onto the side of the truck. There was a little ledge where trash guys stood. We could stand there and ride it out as long as the guard at the entrance didn't see. We would have to dress to blend with the grayish color of the truck. Jack also thought we could crawl under the truck and hold on to something under there. I told him he was a genius. Then he said: Why do you want to escape, anyway? Is it that horrible here? You could end up living in a cardboard box on the street. Henshaw can suck my balls for all I care, but she can't kick me out unless I do something really bad.

I don't know what I want. I'd stay a little longer for that one chick. Jack was all over the place. A new girl appeared yesterday and now he was in love.

The first escape plan would have put Adam and me out on the street and probably in a cardboard box like Jack said. It was a good thing it didn't happen. Jack brought up some good points. I guess I hadn't thought anything through. I was clueless.

Tomorrow Jack would help to keep Henshaw distracted so I could return my file. I risked too much for nothing.

CHAPTER FIFTEEN: SEVEN EXTRA BAGS

A knock at the front door interrupted the story but the disruption was conveniently sandwiched between journal entries. My dad opened the door as I hid the journal behind my back.

"Hi Libby. Hi, kids. What'd you all find out?"

It was Chuck. He was well aware of the journal and was dying to get details. My dad ushered him in the room and told him we were still reading.

"Dad! Oh my God! Did you guys tell everyone?" My dad laughed and led Chuck to his recliner. He allowed Schucker to sit on his throne, but not any of his blood relatives. My mom motioned for me to continue. I wasn't sure I could read in front of Chuck with the flair I mustered for my family.

I took a deep breath and continued.

March 20th, 1986
Everything Changed!!!

The offices emptied at lunchtime as the few bodies that worked there went to the cafeteria to stuff their faces. Some days that was only one person besides Henshaw. My plan was to return my file then. Jack was going to make sure nobody went back to the office until he saw me come to the cafeteria. I grabbed the stack of papers from under my mattress and started to stuff them into my knapsack but I dropped a handful of them. As I was picking them up I saw my birth certificate. I read the lines that listed my parents' names:

FATHER: Matthew Allen

MOTHER: Libby Blackhead

Wait. What!? My birth mother was Emma Allen. My parents were Matt and Emma. Who the hell was Libby Blackhead? It listed her as a resident of Tennessee, USA. Sundown.

"Libby Blackhead is you, mom!" I nervously chuckled in disbelief as my mother gasped and my dad covered his mouth with his hands. We all stared intensely at each other and our eyes fought to pop out of our heads.

"Well, I'll be a rotten tomato!" Chuck said, laughing. "If that ain't some strange coincidence."

"Theo, did you mess with this journal?" I asked the little troublemaker, but he appeared just as shocked as everyone else. "Mom, how could you have a son that lives in another country?" I asked as she walked to the kitchen. My dad leaned back on the sofa and stared at the popcorn ceiling, his mouth hanging open. No one was disputing or arguing this revelation in the slightest. They looked guilty as sin, but it could be an act to punish me for hiding the knapsack. They were teaching me a lesson. I laughed sarcastically. "Ha ha. Real funny."

My mom stood with her back to us and my dad was still trying to catch something in his gaping mouth. Something was too real with the reactions. My parents weren't capable of putting on a show.

"Can someone please say something? Please tell me this is a joke. There has to be another Libby with your name or something, or the information wasn't right in Martin's file," I said. Maybe Theo did narc me out on my pot stash and they were high and this was one amazing practical joke.

"I had an affair," my mom blurted. "It was an accident, okay."

I laughed, unable to fathom the situation. "You're not serious, are you? How do you accidentally have an affair? Did you trip and fall on another man's dick?"

"Don't speak to me like that, Mamie. I put up with enough of your mouth, I don't need it now. I'm not perfect! Is that what you want to hear? Do you want to rub my nose in it like a dog that pees in the house?"

My minimal mathematical and critical-thinking skills were finally being used as I recalled Martin and I were the same age. How could she have both of us at the same time.

"He's your identical twin, Mamie. I am sorry. Your biological father is Martin's dad, Matthew. He was here on business and I met him at the store where I was a supervisor at the time and your father and I were in a complicated place in our marriage. I only slept with him one time, but I got pregnant. Matthew wanted me to get an abortion. He insisted I get an abortion, but I refused. I told him I would raise you both and your dad decided he was okay with that. He wanted me to have you both," she said, delivering this bombshell with a tone that was very matter-of-factly.

I was on an episode of Guiding Light. Every few years on soap operas a missing twin appeared that the other twin knew nothing about. I had a missing twin and my head spun at the notion. Chuck was silent, looking through a Sports Illustrated and wishing he hadn't popped over.

And then my mom started crying uncontrollably. I guessed it a cry of regret. A cry of real loss, knowing her flesh and blood might be dead because he was coming to see her.

"Wow. This is just wow. I don't know what to say," Theo said.

"You don't get to say anything, Theo. Your parents are still your parents. My dad lived in freaking England and died in a frozen creek!" I said as I looked at my other dad. My fake dad, I supposed. It struck me now that we gelled so well because he wasn't my biological father—he was my buddy. He was too calm when it came to disciplining me because he didn't feel comfortable in the father role since he wasn't really my dad. Now it all made sense.

"Okay, then. I should get back to the garden. Those zucchini aren't going to plant themselves, you know," Chuck said as he stood from the throne of the fake father.

"Why did you stay with her?" I asked the man sitting on the sofa across from me, still staring at the ceiling, as my mother cried in the kitchen and Chuck stood uncomfortably, unable to move through the smoky haze of tension.

"Your mother and I really wanted a baby but it just wasn't happening. That's why we were in a bad place in our marriage," he started to explain before my mom chimed in through her sobbing.

"That wasn't the only reason!"

"Yeah, right. I wasn't affectionate enough, either. I didn't buy her candy for Valentine's Day or take her to a fancy restaurant for her birthday, if you can call them reasons. Anyway, when she came to me and told me she was pregnant I felt relieved. It fixed our marriage."

"Yeah, until you found out the kids weren't yours, right?" I asked, still feeling like I was in an episode of The Twilight Zone.

"Honestly, I didn't care."

He was so committed that he accepted and forgave her for cheating on him and getting pregnant by another dude. He loved her so much that he would raise the children as his own. I was too young to believe a love like that even existed.

"Why was Martin given up if Matthew didn't want either of us?"

"Matthew decided he wanted a boy. I'm sorry, Mamie. We didn't know one of you was a boy. The doctor initially misread the ultrasound as two girls. It wasn't until that last ultrasound that he saw a penis. And suddenly he was interested in being a father."

"Why did you agree to give Martin away to that asshole? I mean, he knocked you up and then wanted you to destroy the kids because he thought they were girls. That is sick, mom. Really sick."

"We compromised. It sounds horrible, but I really didn't have any choice. He was the biological father and I couldn't afford a custody battle. Your father and I were happy to have one child at that point. Considering we never thought we'd have any children this seemed like a good compromise at the time. And we never named him Martin, by the way. Our name choice was Gary, Jr."

I laughed. How original, like naming your brown haired dog, Brownie, or your rabbit, Bunny. This answered my next question of why my mother never put two and two together when I was reading the journal. She had no idea Martin was her son.

"Wait, where did I come from, then? Are you my real father?" Theo asked my fake dad. "If you couldn't have kids, how did you have me, then?" The soap opera plot was thickening.

"You were a miracle, Theo," my mom said as Chuck took two more steps towards the door, trying to sneak out unnoticed.

"Oh, he's the miracle and I'm the mistake. How could you do something like this and then go on with life without ever mentioning it or thinking about it again. I mean, you had another flesh and blood child, mom! Did you have no interest in knowing him?"

My mom sat at the table with her back to us and stared out the sliding glass door into the back yard. She sniffled again.

"Yeah, the squash can't very well plant themselves either, so I'm going to head on out. Think it's gonna rain soon anyway. Okay, well, you all have a nice day." Chuck finally got the hell out of an extremely uncomfortable situation. I wanted to do the same. My emotions varied— from anger to sadness with a sprinkle of fear. I needed time alone to process the news in its entirety, but the one aspect that seemed obvious now was why my mom treated me so crappy. She was treating me like the constant reminder of the mistake she made; not just the pregnancy but the affair and the emotional implications that followed. I also understood why she had such harsh viewpoints on sex.

I would need therapy.

And an extra seven bags of pot until I was mature enough to understand and accept and forgive.

"We had an agreement," my dad said as he sat next to me on the floor. "Since the affair caused bunches of stress for both couples, and Gary Jr would be overseas, we would not stay in touch. Mom would make the delivery and we would erase the affair and the other baby from our minds."

"That sounds horrible, and sick, Mamie, but you do what you have to do to keep your sanity," my mom said as she stood and walked back into the living room. "Of course, you can never really erase something like that. But I never looked at him after he was born. That's what the nurses told me to do when they heard he was not going to be mine. I guess it's normal when a woman is a surrogate, that they don't see the baby, they don't hold the baby, they don't form any connection or bond whatsoever, and that's what I did. Instead, I held you, and squeezed you hard enough for the both of you. After Matthew picked up your brother, I never heard from him again. And then depression set in. I can't explain it. I guess I thought it would be easy to fool myself that I only had one baby that day if I didn't see the other baby. And I didn't see him. But I heard him. He cried so hard when he came out. I'll never forget the sound. I can hear it right now. That is the reminder. Every time I came close to forgetting I heard that cry. It's like he knew he wasn't coming home with us, that he wouldn't be part of this family."

Sadness took it's turn and I wanted to cry but I wouldn't let the tears surface. I needed to maintain my strong front of anger for the lies and the deceit and the resentment I felt from my mother. The explanation was sincere and my mother's performance convinced me more than actors on soap operas but I wasn't ready to hand her a daytime Emmy award.

"Mamie, this information doesn't change anything. It doesn't change our family at all. This man sitting here is your father. It doesn't take a birth certificate to make someone a parent, just love and support and nurturing," my mom said.

"It's the truth, sweetheart. I never for a second considered you anyone but my daughter. From the day we brought you home from the hospital."

I needed to hear that. I needed to feel I was indeed special and not an inconvenient accident. "I can't believe you're not my dad. You have been an amazing dad. I have more of a connection to you than I do to mom," I said and then glared at her. "I am never good enough for you, nothing I do ever pleases you. I don't feel loved by you. Like you said, just because someone's name is on a birth certificate doesn't make them a parent." I regretted those words as soon as I heard them leave my mouth. Words can hurt more than a wooden bat with protruding spikes and I knew I needed to be gone from the room for a smoke and a resetting of my emotions.

She sat down again where I sat earlier, eating my cereal in peace before she criticized me, but it was still a normal day then. Nothing seemed normal now. My dad moved to comfort her and I felt evil, like Regan in The Exorcist or Damien's she-devil sister in The Omen. Maybe I was better off in an orphanage like my brother.

"Way to kick mom while she's down, Mamie," Theo whispered in my ear.

"Shut up, half-witted, half- brother."

My parents whispered in the other room and then my dad said, "Please read more from the journal, Mamie." They both returned to the living room with me and half-witted Theo. My mom squeezed my shoulder as she passed and reclaimed her cushion on the sofa. There was a warmth and a weird energy that came from her touch and I almost started wailing like a baby—like Martin did when he was taken away from her.

The story of the adoption overshadowed the discovery of Martin's fate. I opened the journal with a sense of urgency, wishing Devisha was in the audience. She would totally die when I told her I had a twin brother.

MY "MOM" WAS A FAKE MOM, TOO!!!!

I sat back on the bed and thought about my real mother being a woman I never met in the United States. Why was she there? Why didn't I go to stay with her when my parents passed away? And why was I never told about all of this? I dug around in the papers from my file again, looking for any other information. There wasn't anything else that mentioned Libby Blackhead. I read a couple things about my dad and Emma, or mom, I guess I need to respect she was my mother, since she's dead and all. None of the papers had anything about Emma being my adoptive mother or that I was adopted by her. It was time to return the file. I had the name and city of Libby, I thought I would get Marie to help me try to find her. I gathered it all into my knapsack and left my room on the third floor and headed to the office. The coast was clear! Everyone was at the cafeteria. I walked past the counter and to Henshaw's office. The door was closed so I put my ear to it to make sure I didn't hear anyone in there. It was quiet so I grabbed the handle and it turned the whole way. I opened the door and went inside and closed the door behind me. I tried the cabinets to see if they were left unlocked but they were locked so I went to the paper clip drawer at her desk. NO PAPERCLIPS! I looked through all of her desk drawers and couldn't find a single paperclip. I had no way of getting back in the drawer. I WAS SCREWED I thought about just shoving the papers into one of the desk drawers but that would be too obvious. She would know she didn't misplace them like that. I felt defeated. I needed to abort the mission, as I told myself in dramatic fashion. I heard that voice in my head telling me to get the hell out of enemy territory. I turned and walked quickly to the door.

IT OPENED BEFORE I REACHED IT!

Lady Henshaw, in all her glory stood there. No surprised look on her face at all. It was like she was expecting me. Why didn't Jack distract her with another fake choking? Not only did she surprise me, she blinded me in her all-white dress.

The sun was coming through the window behind me and hitting her in a way that gave her a heavenly glow. My backpack was still on my back but I realized I still had the file, or the evidence, in my hand. She stared at it as she slammed, and I mean SLAMMED the door behind her.

I WAS TRAPPED IN HER OFFICE!!!

What happened next was crazy and brutal and I am trying to remember it all perfectly, but I can't.

But it went something like this:

Henshaw started talking first: You can place those documents on the desk, Martin. I do appreciate you returning them. I thought it odd when I pulled out the paperwork of a past resident named Sally from your file yesterday. She was very calm at first. It made me believe things would end okay. What's wrong, dear? Cat have your tongue? Not having much to say would be something unusual for you now, wouldn't it? How did I know you were in here right now?

Well, Martin, your friend, Jack told me all about this. And it wasn't because I threatened him, no. It was all of his doing. He came to me. I was stabbed in the back. But why? What was Jack getting out of this? I told her to fuck off. It just flowed out of my mouth so smoothly it was like I had no control of my speech. She started laughing. Wait a minute. You break into my office, steal confidential files and then curse at me like that? And then she paused for a moment before she started screaming like I've never heard someone scream before. There is something called respect, Martin. You don't damage someone's property and steal from them and then curse at them like they are a piece of garbage, like they aren't the boss of you, like they aren't the LADY of the house! She started walking at me and I backed up. What about my birth mother, I asked. I asked her why she never told me that. I asked her why I didn't just stay with her. She didn't want you, Martin. Nobody wants you, Martin. I couldn't give you to a mad scientist needing organs to create another human!

I laughed and told her that was the stupidest thing I had ever heard. And then she slapped me across the face. I fell to the ground and the knapsack fell off my back. I looked up at her and called her a fucking liar. I asked if she ever called Libby. She kicked me. You're going to the crate. You will be staying in the crate for quite a while! She grabbed me and pulled me up. I reached for my knapsack and my hand must have gone inside the bag by accident, but I ended up pulling out the hunting knife my fake dad got me for Christmas. The sheath fell off it and while I was struggling to get away from Henshaw I stabbed her in the stomach. It wasn't on purpose, I swear. Her eyes got really big and we both looked down at the knife handle sticking out of her belly. I reached for it and pulled it out. She screamed once, but it wasn't very loud. Maybe she couldn't get a deep enough breath to give the scream volume, I don't know, but she fell to the floor, holding her stomach as her white dress started turning red from the blood. I knew this was very bad. So bad. I was going to jail for sure. I knew she would say it wasn't an accident, that I came to her office to kill her.

I put the knife back in the sheath and shoved it back in my bag. Her eyes were open, she was following me with them. I told her I was sorry, that I didn't mean to do it. I told her I would get help and then I left.

I walked out of the office and down the hall not knowing what I was going to do. I couldn't ask for help from anyone. Jack betrayed me. Marie couldn't get tangled up with me or she'd lose everything. I knew I needed to get out of Chatterbee. And then I realized it was Thursday, almost the time for the trash truck to pick up the trash. The Escape Club was a thing once again, only this time I was flying solo. And I could be killed like Rodney, but I had to try. Even though Jack suggested hanging on the outside or underneath the truck I was sure I would be seen, and I couldn't risk not escaping. I headed for the closest exit, which was at the end of the hall, but I would have to pass the two big, open doors of the cafeteria. I walked past fast and I was almost to the exit door when I heard my name behind me.

IT WAS JACK – THE TRADER !!!

Did you put the file back? Is everything okay?

At this point in the story, time was of the essence. If I told him I knew he ratted me out there would be a fight that would keep me from escaping. I told him everything was fine, that I needed to get some fresh air, that I would be back in for lunch.

HE WANTED TO JOIN ME!

I had to quickly play the different options in my head to figure what I should do. I already knew he was in no hurry to escape, so I couldn't invite him along. If I allowed him to go outside with me would I be able to sneak away to the trash truck? And since we talked about it, wouldn't he suspect that was what I was doing? And would he report me to the gate guard? I told him okay, he could join me, but could he run back to the cafeteria and grab me a bottle of water? He said yeah, okay, and headed back as I continued out the door to the parking lot of Chatterbee. I ditched the dickhead that threw me under the bus.

The trash dumpster was around the side of the building and I ran to it. When I got there I was greeted by a friend — BOW!

He had a thick branch in his mouth and I took it from him. It was like he brought it to me to tell me to use it in the back of the truck. To use it to keep the compactor from crushing me like a pancake. He turned and ran to the side of the building and picked up another branch and brought it to me.

THE TRUCK WAS COMING!!!!

I heard it around the corner. I needed to jump in the trash but first I leaned down and kissed BOW on the head and I hugged him, told him he was the greatest, that I loved him and would miss him and I would never forget him. As I stood, my hand got caught in his collar and I accidentally ripped it off. I had no time to mess with it, so I threw it in my bag, said goodbye again as I climbed the side of the trash bin with my knapsack and the two thick branches.

I paused to breathe and looked around the room. The anxiety that I felt was reflected in everyone's faces as our investment in the fate of Martin was now incredibly personal.

He was part of our family.

CHAPTER SIXTEEN: CONNECTING DOTS

I wondered the possibility of twins having a telepathic connection like I'd seen in movies; if they possessed a sixth sense and felt the same things. Could they finish each other's sentences? Was Martin a boy version of me straight down to the curly and frizzy hair? Was he a Little Debbie snack cake addict, too?

"What are you waiting for? What happened to our brother?" Theo asked. I selfishly wanted Martin for myself; he was my identical twin and only a half-brother to Theo. Theo's hands weren't trembling like mine as I held the journal with the answer to Martin's fate. After the shocking revelation I read with curiosity and tension comparable only to Christmas morning, as I unwrapped presents and hoped for the gift I wanted most in the world. I looked to my scabby knees and couldn't believe all that happened in just four short days. I wished I could sneak to my bedroom for a hit to calm my anxiety before I continued the story.

"I never wanted to give up your brother, please believe that. Even after I did, I always hoped that one day I would get to meet him or see him. And I never knew his dad passed away. That Henshaw woman was lying. But I don't understand why I was never notified," my mom said, still processing the information. "I love you both very much," she said through tears. Theo hugged her, his undying support never wavering, of course.

I was much less forgiving—something I would correct later in my life.

The smell was awful in the trash truck. I thought for sure they threw roadkill in there too. I landed on my head and had to gather my bearings very quickly as the metal wall started moving towards me from the side. I really didn't have a solid surface to push off until the wall hit me. I was floating in a lake of trash bags but I held the branches out in front of me and they helped. The wall stopped a few feet in front of me. The stuffed bags actually helped cushion the squeeze.

I WASN'T CRUSHED!

The top of the truck remained open and I was able to hear the gate to Chatterbee closing behind the truck. I was free! Now I just needed to hop the truck at the next stop. I started climbing over the trash and pulled myself up to the opening and waited. Five minutes later I climbed down the side of truck, carefully checking to be sure nobody was watching. I ducked down an alley and hid behind another dumpster as I figured out what I should do next.

March 22nd, 1986

I'm staying in Adam's basement. I waited for him to be outside by himself and I showed myself. He snuck me down and set up a corner. I get to listen to all the ruckus above me. It's a wonder the floor didn't cave in, with his two sisters and brother and mom and dad. I told Adam everything. About Henshaw attacking me and me stabbing her and about how she lied to me about my real mom. I asked him to find out anything about her. Was she okay? Were the police looking for me? Turns out his fake dad is a private eye or detective or something. The basement is big and I'm hidden away in a room on the opposite side from the washer and dryer. Luckily, there is a bathroom down here. It's old and crusty, but it works. Adam sneaks me food down a few times a day. The only other person who ever comes down is Adam's fake mom. THEY ARE NO LONGER FAKE! STOP WRITING THAT! Adam is very happy. He considers them his parents and calls them mom and dad. I am happy for him.

March 23rd, 1986

I was awakened by Adam's dad this morning. Scared the holy hell out of me! He took me upstairs and I sat with the whole family and had breakfast. **IT WAS WEIRD!** Nobody asked me anything or said a word about me or the fact that I was living in their basement. And then everyone left for school and Adam's mom left for work. She's a nurse at the local hospital. I was alone with Adam's dad, named Brent. He started talking. Adam told me everything that went on at Chatterbee. Everything, son. He told me about the punishments and the abuse. He told me you were being beaten by a one Olivia Henshaw and you stabbed her by accident as you were protecting yourself. You aren't in any trouble for this. She never reported you. Oh, yeah, she's alive and well. My wife treated her at the ER. The knife blade missed her organs. I imagine she is not wanting to draw attention to Chatterbee or herself. I also understand you discovered your real mother in the states. He asked to see my files, which I still had in my bag.

He told me he would research and help me find her, but in the meantime I was welcome to stay with them as long as I needed. I finally got to share a room with Adam! And in a much better place.

Brent also pulled Adam and me aside a few days later and told us they were launching an investigation into Chatterbee and Henshaw. They were going back to the death of Rodney and reopening the investigation.

It sounded like they were going to take Lady Henshaw down and shut the place down. This put me in the best mood. I can't remember feeling this happy.

I set the journal down and started to clap and everyone joined me. We were so delighted that Martin finally found a little happiness. I stood and walked in a circle, stretching the cramps from my legs, not sure I wanted to go any further—with only a few pages left, the anxiety in the room was about to boil over like a pot of angel hair pasta.

A knock on the front door ended the storm of reactions and my dad got up to answer. I expected Schucker to stroll in, checking to be sure we hadn't mutilated each other.

It was police officer Howie, another good friend of my dad's.

"Hi Gary. Hi Libby. Do you have a minute?" he asked as my mom joined them at the front door. "Can we go somewhere private," he said. My mom looked at us and back to Howie.

"No. Why don't you come in and have a seat. Please feel free to discuss anything with all of us," she said. Theo and I looked at each other.

"Um, Libby, this is of a highly personal nature, I-"

"We have no secrets, officer. Come on in," she said, seemingly not wanting to keep anything from us ever again.

He walked in the room and looked at my dad with hesitation. My mom motioned for him to sit in the recliner, and he obliged, spinning the damaged chair around to face the entire Blackhead clan. He cleared his throat, removed his hat, and started talking, the first question sending chills down my spine.

"Do you know a boy by the name of Martin Allen?"

My mom lost it. She started crying as she nodded her head.

"Did you find his body? Was he on the plane?" My dad blurted. The tension in the room had reached an unimaginable level, the anticipation of a lit firecracker seconds from exploding.

"I'm afraid so, yes. There was a mix up with names on the plane's manifest and he was listed as Dwight Dunlap, on his way to that outdoor country concert. Dwight was actually on another plane. The remains we found did not match Dwight and it took some digging around to figure out who's they were. When we determined they were Martin Allen's it took even more digging around to find this boy's family. He had no home address, only a previous residence at an orphanage in England, which has been closed. When we finally located the family he had been staying with, we were shared important details of his life including his birth certificate which listed you, Libby, as the mother. Of course, you are already aware of that. Please forgive my invasion of privacy, but we all grew up together and I never knew you had another child."

"Yeah, we didn't know either," I said, the discovery that I had another brother and then didn't have another brother all within hours of time was remarkable and tragic. I hoped for another explanation of how the neon knapsack got on that doomed plane. I hoped Martin was passing through the neighborhood that morning and the knapsack got swept up in the winds of the explosion. I hoped for anything but the awful truth.

"Of course, it's not my business. And whatever the circumstances were, this will stay between us. I'm sorry for your loss."

"Mamie found his knapsack in a tree. She was right under the plane when it exploded," my mom explained. At that point I grabbed the bag and extended it to Officer Howie. He raised his hand to stop the exchange.

"Keep it. We have all the information we need," he said and stood. "Look, I know that this is very difficult to process but it really is a miracle that Martin left this world surrounded by his family; whether or not he knew you all, again, I won't pry into the situation, but it appears you have some of his belongings. What are the odds you would be the one to find the evidence of his life? It absolutely means something and it may take a while to understand. We also located more of his belongings from a storage facility near the orphanage. Would you like them shipped to this address?" My mom nodded and he continued to tell her the sole funeral home in Sundown had Martin's remains and she needed to get with them on a burial.

She cried the hardest I would ever hear her cry in her whole life.

So did I.

CHAPTER SEVENTEEN: THE CEMENT

Officer Howie left and we sat quietly in the living room, my mom's head resting on my dad's shoulder. Her eyes were bloodshot from crying. All of our eyes were a bit swollen from crying except for Theo's. He remained emotionless after hearing the news, which either meant he was still processing the information or he wanted us to leave the room so he could return to destroying the aliens in Space Invaders.

Anxiety over the news spreading through town boiled under the surface and the cliché about small towns rang true: everyone knew each other, and people talked. One funeral home stood in Sundown, owned by the Miller family. If one of the Millers talked to the wrong person everyone would know my mother was an adulterer. She would be branded the town slut and forced to wear cowgirl boots and a plaid shirt with the scarlet letter A. It struck me later that the effects of her infidelity led to her perfectionism. She always struggled to make up for that one time she totally messed up.

I asked to read the last few journal pages aloud but my mom did not want to hear any more of the story of Martin. We knew how it ended. She asked me to place the journal back in the knapsack and hide it away somewhere. The glowing neon green served as a reminder and she wanted the opposite. She wanted to bury the pain, along with the remains of Martin.

I took the journal back to my room and Theo followed.

He closed the door behind us.

"This is the most gnarly thing that's ever happened to us, isn't it? How is any of this even possible," he said as he plopped on my bed so hard the knapsack bounced off and fell to the floor, spilling the contents, including the bloody knife.

"Can you stop being an idiot for once in your pathetic life!" I said and quickly regretted saying it, considering the situation. "Look, yes, this is gnarly."

"Are you still going to call dad, "dad"?"

"Yes. Because he is the only dad I know. Besides, my real dad was an asshole, right? He never wanted me to be born. He was going to have mom get an abortion. That is all I need to know about him. I am gonna forget he ever existed."

"Yeah. He's dead, anyway. It's not like you'd ever meet him. Yeah, everyone that was family seems to be dead right now."

"Can you go in your own room. I need to be alone, okay?"

"No. I'm getting high with you. This seems like the right time for me to try this," he said, knowing my intentions. I rolled my eyes at his nerdy and needy face, sighed, and made him get off the bed so I could grab my goody bag from under it.

"You ever get into this when I'm not here and I'll kick your ass, you hear me?"

Theo nodded and turned on the fan and opened the window. My discretion sucked balls as he knew my tricks. Fortunately, my parents didn't have a clue. I pulled a joint out of the bag and lit it.

The door flew open.

I forgot to stick the yearbook under it. My mom and dad stood in the doorway and suddenly time and everyone froze—the only movement came from the swirling smoke rising from the joint.

"We want in," my dad said, and before I could lie about what was happening, he grabbed the joint from my hand and hit it and passed it to my mom.

"How did you know?" I asked. My mom exhaled and smirked.

"Please, Mamie. Do you think we're fucking morons?"

My mouth dropped at her fuck-bomb and I looked at Theo and we both started laughing. My dad started laughing, too, and my mother soon followed and I couldn't remember the last time I witnessed her laughing at that level. Such heightened emotions ran through our home that day like Speedy Gonzales on his way to a taco stand. We all sat on my tiny twin bed laughing away the horrors of the neon knapsack as the room began to spin.

The ceiling opened, exposing the sunset, and the bed rose from the floor and floated out of the house. We rode that drab bed around town like Angela Lansbury and those homeless kids in Bedknobs and Broomsticks as the four of us became a big block of family cement. One repaired family unit, once fractured but now whole. The closeness and love I felt on that bed with these people was just as intoxicating as the drug. Sharing in the high pushed four family members with nothing in common to a level of contentment only possible with weed. But the effects would wear off and the cement block would begin to crack.

At the vulnerable age of fifteen I discovered the importance of having a healthy balance of family and freedom. That knowledge carried me through to adulthood and while the balance was inconsistent, I never lost the awareness that it required nurturing. My brain on drugs was not only creative, but it was also insightful. A calming and a reflective nature emerged when I was high, and I later got the same feeling from alcohol. My struggles with addiction began out of the necessity to shut off the noise of the world and find inner peace.

Floating through the Sundown air revisited memories we typically only shared while looking at large family pictures on the living room wall from the slide projector. From the time Theo pissed his drawers on The Maid of the Mist at Niagara Falls to the time I was attacked by a swarm of bees and ended up in the hospital and many more traumatic or comical Blackhead rites of passages. An hour later our journey through Sundown and the days of our lives ended as the bed landed back in my room and we curled up with each other and passed out.

Following that tragic and therapeutic day, we made a deliberate effort to appreciate one another. We never turned into The Brady Bunch, where every day was a lesson learned and forgiveness granted, but we never let the periods of anger or struggle linger. A silly laugh or a comment about someone's hair or gathering around the tube for a cheesy horror flick kept that block of cement from eroding too much for the remaining years we spent under the same roof.

"Mom! You got high with mammy and pappy!" Abigail said as I finished the story of the secret sibling. The biggest reaction came from the shared joint and not the existence of an uncle she would never know. I looked at Theo, sitting on the same sofa he did thirty-five years ago, and I could tell he was just as relieved as me to share the story. Losing a brother affected him in a way that required therapy and his medication was song. Over the years he composed songs from Martin's poetry and performed them with his guitar in Nashville.

"Those times we came to your shows you were singing Martin's songs?" Mateo asked.

"Yeah, my original songs weren't entirely original. They were his words and they gave us a sense of who he was. This is how I honor his memory," Theo said.

Merlin's electronic beeping directed us to Sofia, who had discovered the toy from the box of Martin's belongings. I took it from Sofia, feeling protective of Martin's favorite game, and tried to show her how to play but she decided to move on to a stack of plastic hangers in the corner of the room. If Theo connected to Martin through his poetry, then I connected to him through his Merlin and our super powers. When I studied the dates from his journal, I wanted to believe moments existed when sensations took over; chills ran down my spine, or a sudden sadness filled me without explanations, on the same dates.

The morning of the plane explosion I was pushed to the ground by invisible hands on my back. If I hadn't fallen to my knees, I could've lost my head by a piece of airplane metal. Officer Howie said it was special how I found the neon knapsack and I thought Martin could have been a part of everything that happened to me that day.

We all honored Martin in our own ways.

My mother was never slut shamed because the story was altered for the public's consumption. Martin was explained as a distant relative, a long-lost cousin to me and Theo. We never had a public memorial or funeral, but we kept the small amount of his ashes in a house-shaped urn my dad and Chuck made. *(I wondered if their hands ever touched when they built the house.)* The house was modeled after our house and the belief behind the creation was that my brother did make it home. Every night my mother said goodnight to Martin as he rested on the mantel above the fireplace.

That was how my mother honored him.

I don't think she ever pulled the neon knapsack out from the back of my closet, but if she was tempted and read the last few pages of the journal she would've discovered:

April 11th, 1986

I haven't had time to write much anymore. The house is always full and we are always doing something, which is great. It has also helped keep my mind off finding my real mother. Adam's dad told me yesterday that he is still looking. There was no address on the birth certificate and no listings in the phone book for Blackhead. Part of me hopes he can't find her. I'm happy to stay with Adam's family. But it is a cramped house and I don't want to overstay my welcome. Brent also told me they were interviewing boys and girls that had stayed at Chatterbee over the years. He couldn't share with me what they learned from these kids, but he did say there was a case against Henshaw. He asked if I wanted to go into the station to report what I knew. I said NO! I wanted to stay out of it if I could. The Escape plan and the death worried me. I didn't want to end up in another shitty home for kids nobody wanted.

April 15th, 1986

Brent had to go to Mexico for a drug case he was working on. He was still looking for my real mother. I wondered how he could track drug dealers in Mexico but he couldn't find my mother. Maybe he is just trying to protect me. It feels like everyone here likes me living here. Especially Sissy, the older sister. She is 17 and very flirty with me. She is very pretty and I get boners around her sometimes, but I can't do anything with her. That would be bad, I know that.

May 5th, 1986

Brent is back. I missed him. He has really become a father figure to me, and I didn't realize it until he left. He had stitches on his forehead. A work accident he called it, but we knew he got into something bad and dangerous with the drug lords or whoever.

I MADE A HUGE DECISION!!!

I'm staying with Adam's family. Like until I'm of age and then I will move out. I decided I don't want to know or meet my real mother. Why would I even consider it? She gave me up. She was the reason I had such a terrible life. I have happiness now, why would I throw it all away? I consider myself an Evans. MARTIN EVANS at your service. How may I assist you?

May 30th, 1986

Long time, no speaky. Things are great. I went back to school a few weeks ago. My staying with the Evans family is legal now or something. I'm not adopted or anything, but legal guardians, I think.

CHATTERBEE IS SHUT DOWN!

LADY ASS SNIFFER IS GOING TO JAIL!

Adam and me got drunk to celebrate. The rest of the family went shopping and we stayed home and raided the booze. I probably won't do it again. I didn't really like the head spins, and I'm pretty sure Brent knew, even though we hid in the bedroom that night.

June 4th, 1986
I Lost

I was home sick from school. I was in bed. Sissy, who was done with school for the year because she was graduating and finished with classes, came in to check on me. She put her hand on my forehead. "You are so hot," she said, and not in a nurse kind of way, but in a I want your body kind of way. I was too weak to fight her roaming hand. She stuck it under the sheets and before I knew it she was on top of me and riding me like a wild stallion. It felt amazing, and I really didn't have to do anything. I lost my virginity. Even though it was great, I felt a little molested. But do boys argue about it? Or be happy about it? I was happy, yet scared about the family finding out. Sissy promised she wouldn't tell anyone.

June 6th, 1986

Brent took me out on the back porch after dinner for a private chat and I was sure he knew I screwed his lovely daughter. I was ready to be shipped out to somewhere else. Instead he told me he found my mother. And he also told me I had an identical twin sister. I cried. Not sure where the emotion came from, but I felt like I had missed out on so much. I felt abused yet again, this time by the woman who pushed me out of her body. I had a sister, a real, flesh and blood sister that I was denied. I was pissed. I wanted to meet her. Them. Both, I wanted to go to the United States of America. To the state of Tennessee. Brent not only understood, he said he would get tickets and that he would take me to meet them. He wouldn't leave me with them, though. He knew it was important for me to meet them but not expect to be a part of their lives.

June 10th, 1986
The Flight

I'm on the plane writing in this book. I am alone. Brent and I were on the way to the airport when he got a call from his chief or boss. They needed him to go back to Mexico, they located a drug dealer. He was going to take me home but I begged him to let me fly alone. I knew what to do. I read about it at the library a couple days ago. I was an adult, I told him. I could do it. I am flying to a city called Knoxville tonight and catching a smaller plane in the morning to the town of Sundown. Heading to Sun-down at Sun-up. I hugged Adam and the rest of the Evans' and Sissy kissed me on the cheek, which I played off in front of everyone, like it was gross. But I got a boner, of course. That thing between my legs had a mind of its own. I am scared to meet Libby and my sister, Mamie. I'm having second and third thoughts about this trip. If I'm only going out of anger, what is the point? I think deep down, I want to be welcomed with open arms and love. Many apologies and begging for forgiveness and begging for me to stay and be part of their family.

WHAT A FANTASY!

This isn't Dynasty! This is real life and my life has been so real that other people couldn't handle it. Actually, my life would make a great television show. It would blow Dynasty out of the water! It's weird looking out the window of this plane, my first time flying. It's dark but I can see lights way down below, coming and going. I brought two of my favorite cassette tapes, Duran Duran and INXS. My headphones will get me through the travel part of this adventure, and when I let my brain start to worry, I think about all that I've already been through in my life and I tell myself that this is a piece of bloody cake. Not literally bloody cake, more of a five-layer chocolate cake with white icing on the outside and fudge icing between the layers. Headphones ON!

"'Cause when all the curtains are pulled back we'll turn and see the circles we've traced..."

Martin was the last one to leave the house. Three months of boxing, selling, and trashing the innards of the family home had come to an end. On the eve of the Blackhead house hitting the real estate publications I grabbed that model house and the remains of my identical twin and we took a trip to the city of storytellers and dreamers. Music City and Theo awaited us and the approach to the big city lights gave me a satisfying sense of closure to several chapters of my own journal. Some chapters should've ended decades ago while others required editing before turning the last page.

Sitting in the cramped bar off the main drag with my children, listening to one brother sing the words of another brother, was the cherry on top of a cathartic hot fudge sundae. For once in my life being surrounded by alcohol in a bar did not cause me to sweat with anxiety for even though the world was noisy I had enough inner peace to last me the rest of my sobriety pregnancy.

And beyond.

Leaving

Is it true that life can become new?
That the world can offer another road
That the sky can offer another sun
That the universe can offer another star?
Sometimes you have to leave the things you know
Sometimes you have to give away and dissolve -
like a cold winter's snow
The people and the love that helped you and your climb
like steps on a ladder
Now will continue to support your next adventure
The next chapter
A complete reset and do-over with more knowledge
to do it better a second time. Or a hundredth time.
Did it really matter how many times?
I'm leaving.
On a plane.
I have found the next rung on my ladder.

THE END

ABOUT THE AUTHOR

Michael Evanichko knew he wanted to write from a young age while growing up in western Pennsylvania. Reading the schlocky horror novels from the eighties ignited his warped imagination and prompted his first attempt at penning a novel at age twelve. His passion for writing was the foundation for all his creative endeavors, culminating with the completion of his first full-length, mainstream novel, *Life in a Supermarket Basket*. His follow-up novel, *Life in a Savage Landfill*, continues the story of a pivotal character from *Supermarket Basket*. The third novel in **The Trilogy of Life**, *Life in a Neon Knapsack*, also includes a character from the first two novels. Michael currently lives in Tennessee, where he sometimes plays with the deer and antelope.

MichaelEvanichko.com

Life in a Savage Landfill | Facebook

Life in a Supermarket Basket | Facebook

www.imdb.com/name/nm0262493/?ref_=fn_al_nm_1

instagram.com/mich2evanichko/